TRACERS

TRACERS

J.J. HOWARD

G. P. PUTNAM'S SONS
AN IMPRINT OF PENGUIN GROUP (USA)

G. P. PUTNAM'S SONS
Published by the Penguin Group
Penguin Group (USA) LLC
375 Hudson Street
New York, NY 10014

USA | Canada | UK | Ireland | Australia
New Zealand | India | South Africa | China
penguin.com
A Penguin Random House Company

Library of Congress Cataloging-in-Publication Data
Howard, J. J. (Jennifer Jane), 1972–
Tracers / J. J. Howard.   pages cm
Summary: "Cam is a New York City bike messenger with no family or strings attached to anyone, but when he meets a mysterious stranger and is pulled into her dangerous world of parkour, he is torn between following his heart and sacrificing everything to pay off his debts"—Provided by publisher.
[1. Parkour—Fiction. 2. Love—Fiction. 3. Criminals—Fiction. 4. Orphans—Fiction. 5. New York (N.Y.)—Fiction.] I. Title.
PZ7.H83296Tr 2015   [Fic]—dc23   2014031563

Printed in the United States of America.
ISBN 978-0-399-17373-8
10 9 8 7 6 5 4 3 2 1

Design by Annie Ericsson.
Text set in Warnock Pro.

For my mom and dad.

Meet you at Warren's to celebrate.

TRACERS

PROLOGUE

HE KNEW the stars were up there somewhere, but with all the lights from the city, Cam couldn't see them. He sat on the edge of the roof waiting for her. Looking down at the little toy car he held, Cam realized he didn't even remember bringing it with him, but there it was, clutched in his hand— so hard that the small wheels made indentations in his palm. Once, long ago, his father had given him the toy, a miniature of the black GTO he drove, along with the promise that one day Cam would inherit the real thing.

He reached into his back pocket and pulled out the picture—one of the only ones he had of his family. The photo he *did* remember bringing up here. He'd had to search around for it—wasn't like he carried it around with him. Why would he? Just like the seemingly starless New York City sky, the picture was a lie. There, frozen for a moment in time, was his family: his father, smiling, with an arm slung around his pregnant wife. They stood leaning against the life-size version of the toy Cam held in his hand. Anyone looking at his parents' hopeful faces in the photo would think they were going to be together . . . build a life. Maybe even be happy.

A lie.

"You look like your dad," said a voice in his ear.

Nikki sat down beside him.

Cam didn't answer. He closed his eyes, for that moment just feeling the warmth of her next to him.

She went on, her voice low. "I don't even know my real dad . . ." She trailed off, and her hand found his. "I don't even know what he looks like," she told him, a catch in her voice. She leaned her head against his shoulder.

With his free hand he held the picture out to her and she took it from him. He exhaled, then felt the words start to escape from him. For some reason he felt the urge to go confessional around her. It was a new and uncomfortable feeling.

"*My* dad was a guy I talked to on a phone through a glass

window . . . he was a lowlife thrill seeker." Cam swallowed hard, ignoring the voice in his head telling him to shut up.

Not that he was one to share much of anything, but he *never* talked about his father to anyone. Ever. With Nikki around, suddenly *never* had started to turn into *sometimes*.

When it came to Nikki, what he really wanted, though, was *always*.

He went on: "When I was ten, my dad panicked while he was robbing a liquor store in Queens." Cam felt Nikki's hand tighten around his. "He shot an old man for fifty-seven bucks and change. Someone stabbed him to death in prison because he stole their cigarettes."

Cam took the picture back from her and shoved it in his pocket. Nikki had pulled her head away from his shoulder. She was staring at him. Her eyes were wet, but she didn't cry.

"Sometimes it's better not to know," he said.

The toy car was still there in his hand. He stared down at it, thinking about the real GTO. Thinking about escape. And though for the moment he'd mastered the urge to spill every thought and hope and fear he'd ever had to her, she still figured it out.

"You're leaving," she stated, her voice flat. "Aren't you?"

Cam let go of her hand, only to put his arm around her

waist and pull her closer. He stared at her for a few seconds. Her eyes were almost silver in the moonlight, and still full of tears. One blink and she'd be crying. He nodded slowly.

She blinked.

Cam pulled her even closer to him, and lowered his forehead to hers, hearing her breath, as ragged as his own. "Come with me," he whispered.

"I can't . . ." she whispered back, another catch in her voice.

"Don't think. Just . . . come with me."

Nikki pulled a little away from him. She wiped her eyes and opened her mouth to speak—but before she could tell him all the reasons she couldn't leave this place, he needed to tell her one more thing.

"I know what you're going to say. You're going to tell me your brother needs you, that Miller won't let the two of you—won't let *any* of us—go." Cam pulled her back to him, holding on tight. She didn't push him away. "But Nikki, I'm telling you. I don't care. I don't care if any of that's true—or if it's all true. Because ever since you fell out of the sky and crashed into my life, the only thing I care about is you. I'm not leaving without *you*."

He let her go, stood up, and held out his hand.

They both knew that they could never be together, that they'd never find a way out. But Cam told himself it didn't matter.

If everything else in his life had been a lie, she was the truth. The way he felt about this girl, in this moment. *That* was true.

He took a deep breath and waited . . .

FIFTEEN DAYS AGO . . .

ONE

AND A MOMENT of silence for the bike.

Crushed under a bus: what a way to go. This wasn't how Cam's day was supposed to play out, although he'd stopped expecting much of anything—good, anyway—a long time ago. The morning had started like any other: hot run, bike whizzing through the cars and taxis like they were standing still, back to Lonnie for another pickup.

As usual, Cam had sailed right through the wide door at the front, past the other messengers jockeying for a pickup.

"You got a run?" one of them asked Lonnie. It was probably Mitchell—sounded whiny enough to be him. But Cam didn't stop to find out.

"I got a run for *Cam,*" Lonnie shot back, and held up the

slip. "Express run. Uptown. I need . . ." But Cam had already grabbed the slip. He was back on the pavement, legs pumping, air rushing past him as he pedaled.

Cam put in his earbuds and cued up some music on his phone. The volume was cranked to the max, but he could still hear the sounds of the traffic he sailed through. Somebody like that Mitchell kid would probably have those noise-canceling earbuds—that guy didn't actually *need* to work for Lonnie. Not when his shoes cost more than Cam's rent. The guy just liked to be able to tell his hipster friends in Brooklyn that he was a bike messenger—even though he spent most of his time sitting around on the couch in the break room.

Don't think about money. It wouldn't help anyway. All Cam could do was keep riding faster. Sometimes it felt like that was all he ever did.

Cam rode through the chaos of morning traffic without slowing—down the center, riding right between the yellow lines, weaving his way between the cars and people, then jamming a left, catching the slipstream of a crosstown bus. He caught onto the side, taking a rest and letting the bus do the work. Most of the passengers were reading, headphones on, tuned out. But one old lady's eyes widened. Cam grinned.

He spotted a yellow light just ahead, let go of his free ride, and then it was a slingshot through the intersection. Cam jumped a curb for the next shortcut, and hitched another ride with a beat-up old Civic.

And then a guy in a hoodie dropped out of the freaking sky, smack in the middle of the traffic snarl. He must have jumped from above, but it sure as hell looked like he'd just dropped out of nowhere. He landed on the roof of a car, then jumped down into the street. A cab swerved to miss him.

Over the music blasting through his crap headphones, Cam heard the cab's tires squeal. Smelled the burning rubber.

The cab was sliding sideways toward him, fast. He was boxed in; with nowhere to go, Cam turned his bike sideways at the last second, sliding over the back end of the cab, his body crashing into the metal. It wasn't his first full-body slam into a moving vehicle, but it was the hardest hit he'd taken so far. He could feel the impact of the metal jar his bones, and his body was twisting in midair, 180 degrees and then down, landing with a thud on top of the guy in the hoodie.

No, wait . . .

It definitely *wasn't* a guy. Cam froze. She froze. Her face was inches away from his. They were both breathing hard. Her silver-blue eyes locked with his for what must have been just a few seconds, but it seemed longer.

The sound of the bike's final moments broke the spell—it had skidded sideways out from under him, landing in the perfect spot to be crushed under the wheels of the M14 bus—and Cam realized she was struggling to push him off her. He rolled away, lying on his back on the pavement and cradling his left arm, which felt like it was on fire.

"Are you okay?" she asked, as she struggled to her feet. Her hood had slipped down. Cam looked up and took in his first full view of her: long brown hair, ripped jeans.

"Yeah. I'm fine," he managed to say.

But she'd already turned away. Her eyes were on the ground—she was searching for something, and still breathing hard. Maybe dropping out of the sky hadn't been quite as easy as she'd made it look.

Cam managed to stand, avoiding putting any weight on his damaged left arm.

He forced himself to stop staring at her. She was insanely pretty, which made it difficult to tear his eyes away. But pretty girls weren't anything new. They were always chasing after him. This girl was something else, though.

Something more. Or maybe he was just impressed with her dramatic entrance.

He spotted a messenger bag in the gutter that must have belonged to her, and went over to pick it up.

Before he could make the most of his white-knight moment, she snatched the bag out of his hands and turned to go.

"You're welcome," Cam said, and she met his eyes again. After hearing how not-welcoming his voice sounded, she frowned.

Unfortunately, frowning didn't make her any less hot.

She'd killed his bike, and to top it off: rude.

But still. Hot.

Cam realized she'd just asked him a question.

"Are you sure you're okay?" she repeated.

He stared at her. "I don't know." And it was true. Between her dropping out of the sky, turning out to be a gorgeous mystery girl, *and* the small matter of his body getting slammed into a cab—hard—Cam was dazed as well as confused. He glanced up at the five-story building behind him. She must have jumped down from the roof. (*How?* was a good question—and also *why?*)

Cam shook himself and saw that the girl was still staring

at him, but then she spotted two cops headed toward them. "Sorry about your bike," she said, as she whipped her hood back on and ran off.

Crazy girl ran a few steps *up* the side of the nearest building, barely avoiding a gaggle of tourists, and dropped down into the subway entrance.

One of the cops actually shrugged. Chase over.

Cam stood staring at the entrance to the F train, closing his own mouth. He didn't want to look like one of the tourists. After all, he'd lived here his whole life.

But he'd never seen a girl drop out of the sky.

Cam made his way back to work—walking, thanks to a very strange girl and a last-minute assist from a crosstown bus. When he got back, he looked around Lafayette Messenger Service. He wasn't sure he'd actually *walked* in since his first day on the job—the messengers' entrance was a wide garage door, with a concrete floor so the riders could coast right in without wasting any time. Since Cam was moving at about a tenth his usual speed, he noticed things he usually ignored. And, wow, the place was a crap hole when you really slowed down to look. The floor was crisscrossed with spray paint and various other stains. A couple of armchairs, probably from the seventies, were held together with duct tape. A bank of yellow lockers filled the back wall, some with missing doors, the rest scribbled over with doodles and curse words. The remaining walls had been "decorated" by Lonnie's ex-girlfriend, who liked to take extreme-close-up photos of completely random things like artichokes or dog noses. Word had it she'd left him for a Williamsburg hipster who managed not to roll his eyes when she called her stuff "art." Lonnie had been in a rotten mood ever since.

The other messengers were giving Cam curious looks—no doubt because he was carrying the remains of his bike. Or maybe this was how they always looked at him, but he was usually moving too fast to notice. Cam ignored them. He walked up to the front counter and handed Lonnie the envelope he'd been sent uptown to deliver. When Lonnie opened his mouth to complain, Cam laid what was left of his Fantom on the front counter. Lonnie swore under his breath and took the envelope back from him. With a sigh, Cam pushed open the door to the break room. He threw himself down on the couch and closed his eyes.

"Are you just gonna leave this mess here?" Lonnie yelled after him, but Cam didn't respond.

His arm was still on fire, and the rest of his body ached

as well, but he couldn't stop thinking about what he'd seen that girl do.

He might have assumed her first dramatic jump was a failed suicide attempt or something. But the way she'd moved like a cat, or maybe a monkey—up the wall, over the bench, and down into the subway—that had to be parkour. He pulled out his phone to look it up. *Spelling* it was a whole other issue. But even when he missed the *u*, hundreds of results came up on YouTube. One of the first ones showed two guys dressed like Mario and Luigi running around like they were inside a video game, but Cam clicked past it. Their movements were jerky, not fluid like hers had been.

The next guy was full of advice. Like: don't snap your Achilles tendon. Okay, good tip.

Cam went searching for a new clip, since this guy mostly seemed to want to talk for half an hour about a move rather than actually *doing* the move.

He kept clicking. The running-up-the-wall move was called a tic-tac, Cam learned.

He watched two tiny figures running through a park, vaulting up and off trees, leaping over benches. It looked like Riverside Park, but the image was too small to be sure. The wild tricks the tiny figures were performing might have seemed unreal, except Cam had seen with his own eyes—the girl had performed several of the tricks that very morning.

One of the clips Cam clicked on had a tagline: "No equipment necessary." Sounded like the perfect sport for him, since he couldn't afford any. He also found out that the sport was called, variously, parkour, tracing, or free running. He liked the last one best: anything with *free* in the name sounded great to Cam. He'd felt trapped for so long.

Then it hit him that, given the way his life was turning out, learning how to run faster and more efficiently through the obstacle course of the city could actually come in pretty freaking handy someday.

Plus he had a background in martial arts, which a few of the videos mentioned as being helpful. He wasn't afraid of heights, or falling, or much of anything really. After all, he'd seen his share of trouble—even spent six months in medium security up in Otisville. Maybe he'd take a crack at it himself when his arm got better. Why not?

He was distracted by Lonnie's voice, booming from the garage. "Washington Heights. Express run."

Mitchell stuck his head into the break room and grinned down at Cam before going up to the front desk. Cam snorted when he saw the guy was attempting dreadlocks. "Later,

Cam," he said with a smirk. His blond wannabe-dreads bounced as walked back toward the counter.

Cam rolled his eyes, closed out of YouTube, and leaned back against the ancient couch cushions, closing his eyes.

A bike messenger with no bike. This was the best day ever. There weren't many people who would hire a guy with a record, so his options were pretty limited. Sometimes he felt like he'd never be done paying for the mistakes he'd made when his mother got sick.

"You want your check or not?" Lonnie's voice pulled him back from the edge of sleep.

His boss was standing in front of him, his frown looking even more pronounced than usual. Lonnie's light brown eyes looked tired, and the black Lafayette Messenger Service polo he always wore hung loosely off him. Cam felt bad for Lonnie—his ex had really done a number on him.

Cam sighed and heaved himself upright, grabbing the check. And then he went from feeling bad for Lonnie to feeling bad for himself. The envelope, once opened, contained a check for a disappointing $493.

He waved the envelope in front of the dispatcher's eyes. "This is it? I need more runs, Lonnie."

Lonnie sighed. "Uh, Cam? You need a *bike*. You're my

best rider. What am I gonna do?" He nodded toward the remains of his bike, which were still decorating the dispatch counter.

"Yeah." Cam frowned. "It really sucks . . . *for you.*"

Cam's eyes followed his boss's to the bike corpse. Wasn't like he'd been expecting a banner day or anything. But still.

"Got a friend who can loan you one?" Lonnie asked.

Cam's eyes ran over the crew of messengers ignoring him *and* the remains of his dearly departed Fantom. Not likely they'd be sympathetic about this one. More likely they'd be psyched about not losing any more runs to him.

"What's it look like to you?" Cam said, hearing the bitterness in his own voice. He scooped up the broken bike frame, hoisted it over his shoulder, and walked out.

He joined the throng of people moving on the sidewalk, and his thoughts shifted to the guys jumping and running in the last video. That seemed like an infinitely better way to get around. But he still needed a bike to make runs for Lonnie, and get paid. Cam started mentally doing the math on how much he owed . . . and what he *wasn't* going to make over the next few days, bikeless.

It was all hoodie girl's fault. Maybe he could find her, let her know how screwed he was now because of her.

He passed a Dumpster and threw the remains of his bike inside; it was broken beyond repair.

Now he could just go find hoodie girl. That was a solid plan. Start on the F train and then walk all over the city looking for a girl with silver eyes who ran up walls, so he could give her a piece of his mind.

At least he'd gotten the walking part right. Because now: pedestrian.

Cam swore under his breath and kept walking.

TWO

THE SIGN said CHECK CASHING but it probably should have said check swiping. Because infesting the sidewalk right by the entrance were Cam's two least favorite people: Jerry and Hu.

Chinatown's finest: Chen ran the books, but Jerry and Hu were the ones who finessed the situation. *Finesse*—that's what Jerry liked to call it. Hu mainly just grunted—he was the muscle. Built like a tank.

Cam stared at Hu in his sleeveless black shirt and imagined the guy trying to run up a wall. Then imagined him hitting the pavement. Hard. It was *almost* a comforting thought.

Except for the fact that Jerry had just grabbed the paycheck right out of his hands.

"How did you . . . ?" Cam sputtered.

"How'd we know it was payday?" Jerry grinned and tapped his forehead. "I did some research, my friend. Your boss was pretty chatty." Jerry gave Cam a pointed look. "As for the rest of it, this is the closest and most convenient check-cashing place. Didn't take a rocket scientist."

"Luckily," Cam spit out, before he had time to think it over. He was pissed off about being ambushed. He would have turned most of his pay over to them anyway. But it might have been nice to hold on to a few bucks for, you know, food.

Jerry responded with a smile, but it wasn't a nice one. "It's your fault, me having to play Sherlock, Cam. Where have you been hiding?" Hu just glared and cornered Cam against the building. Jerry stepped closer too, still smiling his oily smile. "You didn't forget about us, did you?"

Cam met Jerry's eyes. He kept his voice even. "I didn't forget. I didn't have the money."

"What do you call this?" Jerry waved the paycheck in front of Cam's nose. "So what else you got?" Jerry put out his hand. Cam resisted the urge to spit his gum right into Jerry's waiting palm.

Jerry was taller than Hu, and skinnier. He also seemed

to be pretty obsessed with his hair: he wore it long in the front, but gelled into perfect waves. Jerry took another step forward, reaching into Cam's pockets.

"Come on, man . . ."

Soon Jerry had his wallet. A few seconds later he'd emptied it of its contents: two fives. Jerry flung the empty wallet back at Cam.

"That's it? Where's all your money going?"

Cam spoke through clenched teeth. "To you."

"You came to *us* for a loan, Cam. You accepted the terms. Remember? Fifteen hundred on the first of the month. *Every* month."

"You're right. My bad. I'm sorry I missed the payment." He swallowed hard, still staring into Jerry's eyes. "It won't happen again."

"No, it won't." Jerry pulled a pen out of the interior pocket of his jacket. The lining was a shiny red material printed with little gold dragons. Cam's eye roll was automatic, no stopping it.

Jerry didn't catch it, or pretended not to. "Sign this."

"But, Jerry . . . I gotta pay rent."

Jerry was shaking his head. Looking almost like he gave a damn. Almost.

"Think I'm doing this for fun, kid? This is my job. I got a boss just like you do. Sign it."

Hu grunted as if to add his encouragement. Cam took the pen and endorsed the check. Jerry folded it, put it in his pocket, and stepped away from the wall. Cam followed, and Jerry put a hand on his shoulder. "We like you, man. We really do. But this is the second time you've been late."

Hu made another sound—this one more of a growl.

Jerry fixed his eyes on Cam. "Second time," he repeated. "And that makes us nervous."

Cam frowned as Jerry gave him one more shoulder pat. "You owe us fifteen *thousand* dollars, Cam. Plus interest. Don't miss another payment."

"I won't."

Cam watched them head inside.

Jerry turned back to Cam and mouthed through the glass: "Don't miss another payment."

Yeah, because watching Jerry cash *his* paycheck was really making it easy to forget.

The L train wasn't late, which was his first piece of "luck" all day.

But then there was the fact that the left side of his

earbuds had crapped out—no doubt more fallout from the madness that morning. Cam pulled the cord out of his phone and threw them across the almost-empty train.

He rode in silence, staring at the subway map above his head. The L went from Eighth Avenue to Canarsie, and back again. It seemed like a perfect metaphor for his life: riding a train that didn't actually *go* anywhere—just an endless loop.

Like the tattoo of an infinity symbol he'd gotten after his mom died. It was inked in stark black on his left shoulder. At the time it had seemed like a comforting idea—that maybe everything in life was some kind of continuous loop, a cycle of birth and death, happiness and suffering. But now the ink just seemed depressingly symbolic.

When had everything started to go so wrong? What if his dad had picked a different store to rob? Or never pulled that gun? What if his mom hadn't gotten sick?

Was there a moment when he could have gone left instead of right? If he'd never taken the loan . . .

Cam thought back to the time when Chinatown was just another neighborhood to him—before he'd even known what the name *Tong* meant. Of course he'd always known that Chinatown was *organized*, but until he'd been desperate to borrow money fast, he hadn't needed to know anything more.

He'd been making deliveries to a restaurant on Canal Street every few days ever since he started working for Lonnie. It had been obvious from the start that the well-dressed guys who met every night in the back weren't waiters or cooks, so one night Cam worked up the courage to ask about a loan . . . and the rest was history. The Tong, he found out later, was a *particularly* well-organized group—especially when it came to making sure all debts were paid in full. If only he could go back and do things differently . . .

But it was no use wondering about that. The fact was his mom *had* gotten sick. And they'd needed the money— period. Just like he needed money now.

An image of the girl with the silver eyes appeared in his mind, seemingly from out of nowhere, just like she'd shown up that morning. Cam shook his head to banish her from his brain.

Even if he found her—*and* decided to forgive her for ruining his day, and his bike—right now he didn't even have the funds to buy her a hot dog.

None of it mattered. Thinking about the mystery girl was just a waste of time, like showing up for work tomorrow (bikeless) would be. She'd made him curious was all. He would never see her again.

◆ ◆ ◆

Cam trudged the five blocks from the L station to Angie's row house. Home sweet home: peeling gray paint, rusted bars on the windows. But all this luxury wasn't for Cam—since it was the *garage* he rented from Angie, not an actual room.

Not too many folks were keen on renting to someone like him—and even fewer were willing to skip the credit check and accept the rent in cash. But Angie had worked with his mom a long time ago. She was one of the few people who'd come to her funeral. When she'd asked if he had a place to stay—after the bank had taken the house—he'd been too depressed and defeated to lie. So he'd ended up in her garage. The rent was cheap; sometimes she even brought him leftovers. Angie's stew, mac and cheese, and lasagna were the only things he ever ate that didn't come on a stick or wrapped in paper or plastic. He never turned down her offerings. Cam hated feeling like a charity case, but he was starting to hate fast food even more.

Angie's kid, Joey, was pulling tricks on his skateboard in the driveway—as always, he looked like he was one sneeze away from a trip to the emergency room.

Just at that moment, the kid wiped out, sent his board flying in Cam's direction. Cam stopped it with his foot.

"You all right?" he asked as he kicked the skateboard up and caught it.

"Yeah. I'm good." Joey cocked his head to one side. "Hey, where's your bike?"

Not much got by Joey—the kid was observant as hell. Cam had never had a little brother, but he imagined the way he felt about Joey probably fit into the little-brother category. Equal parts affection and annoyance.

"I hit a pothole," Cam lied, turning the board over to inspect the wheels. "Looks like you got bigger problems. Come on." He led the way into the garage and through the maze of car guts.

The garage was perfect for Cam—just enough room for the car and all his tools. He didn't have much else. His living space was in the back corner: twin bed covered in a flannel blanket. (In his head, his mom's voice still told him to make the bed every morning.) He kept a plastic crate next to it, topped with a lamp, clock radio, and a couple of books. Another crate turned on its side was his "closet"; he kept his T-shirts, jeans, and cargos neatly stacked inside. His winter gear—a couple of sweatshirts and a heavier coat and scarf—was stored under the bed.

Joey perched on the edge of a stool, picking up a toy car from the workbench. He held it up and spun the wheels of the miniature '67 GTO, but his eyes were on the life-size version that took up most of the garage. "When can we go for a ride?" he asked.

Cam stood before the workbench, tightening the trucks on Joey's skateboard. "Doesn't run yet, kid. Haven't had time to work on it." He switched screwdrivers and kept tightening. "Don't have money for the parts I need," Cam added, talking mostly to himself.

"Maybe you should sell it," Joey said, still spinning the wheels on the toy.

"Maybe." Cam looked over at the car. He didn't have the energy to explain that even though his dad hadn't been worth a damn, Cam wanted . . . *needed* to hold on to his car.

He handed the skateboard back. "You're good to go."

"Thanks, Cam." Joey returned the toy GTO and Cam put it in his toolbox. He buried it a little under a hammer and a chunk of exhaust pipe.

"Joey?" Angie was calling. When he didn't appear, she showed up at the garage door. "I told you to give Cam his space." She frowned.

Joey rolled his eyes. "Chillax, Mom. It's all gravy." Joey threw down his board, hopped on, and sailed back down the driveway. Cam couldn't help but smile.

"Seems like just yesterday he was so cute and little. And

now . . . so full of attitude." Angie turned back to Cam. She looked tired—and much older than she actually was. There were always dark circles under her eyes. "Sorry about that . . ."

She looked like she was in the perfect mood to hear some more bad news.

"I don't mind," Cam told her. "He's a good kid."

He took a deep breath and let it out. It was no use putting it off. It wasn't like he was getting any richer sitting here fixing Joey's board or his old man's wreck of a car. "Listen, Angie . . . I'm going to be a little late with the rent this month. I'm sorry." He swallowed hard; seeing Angie do her best to smile at him was like a knife twisting in his gut. He felt bad enough already. "I'll get it to you as soon as I can. I swear . . ."

Angie sighed, and it seemed to shake her thin frame. "I know you're good for it, Cam. But I'm having a tough month. Just . . . promise to try your best, okay?" Angie's eyes were dark brown, but they seemed faded somehow. Like even at thirty-five she'd already seen way too much. She always reminded Cam of his mom, even though he'd never seen the two of them together, and they certainly looked nothing alike. Angie was African American, about a head taller than his mom had been. Maybe, Cam thought, it was the way Angie had about her: she was so tired and sad—but she wasn't broken. That part definitely reminded him of his mom.

Cam tried to muster a reassuring smile for her. "Promise. Thanks, Angie."

He watched her go, looking around the garage at everything he owned. It was actually sort of depressing how easily his possessions would fit into the trunk of the GTO.

Which would be entirely pointless unless the car actually *ran*.

Feeling possessed all of a sudden, Cam stood up and started rooting through all his workbench crap until he found it: *Chilton's Repair and Tune-up Guide: Pontiac GTO 1965–68*.

His earbuds were now part of the garbage slime on the floor of the L train, but luckily he had a speaker hidden somewhere on the bench.

He'd had the same song stuck in his head all day—ever since *she* had jumped down from the sky like some lunatic cat. Cam wasn't usually that choosy about the music he played. His dad, on the other hand, had been obsessed with music—he'd loved seventies rock the most, but Cam remembered him listening to everything. When he was little, his dad always made mix CDs for the stereo in the GTO. He always said he was making a road-trip mix, but Cam couldn't remember a time when they'd actually *gone* anywhere.

For Cam, music had always just been noise—a way to drown out the city. Dance and techno—anything with a driving beat—created the best wall of sound. Usually when he worked on the car he just set the music on his phone to shuffle and let it play.

But today Cam opened up Pandora and created a new station based on the song playing on repeat in his brain: Bad Company's "Ready for Love." His dad had kept the band's CD in the GTO when Cam was a kid—God only knew where it had gone. Cam had a vague memory of riding in the backseat, closing his eyes as the sunshine streamed in through the open windows, and letting the music wash over him.

He connected his phone to the speaker. The beauty of living alone in a crummy garage was that no one was around to judge his embarrassing music choice, so Cam cranked the volume and sang along: "Wonderin' where my life is leading . . . Rollin' on to the bitter end . . ."

Such a good question, Cam thought to himself. Where *was* his life leading?

He kept singing through the chorus: "I want you to stay . . ." And for some reason it was *her* he was singing about . . . *she* was the one he was singing to.

Even though he—and his Fantom—had been crushed because of her, he still couldn't get the mystery girl out of his brain. When he closed his eyes, Cam could see every detail of her face like she was standing right there in front of him—but mostly those eyes. They were such a light, clear, silvery blue . . . he'd never seen anyone with eyes like that.

It was funny. Just like music, faces were usually background to him. He was used to streaking past thousands of faces every day. He was always pushing as hard as he could to speed past everyone and everything, because he didn't belong to anybody, and nobody belonged to him. The faces were interchangeable. He never slowed down to look.

Until she showed up.

Well, jumped *down*.

In his distracted state, Cam hadn't realized he'd pulled off the GTO's radiator cover and removed the AC belt. Now that he'd come this far, he might as well replace the serpentine belt like he'd been meaning to. It was a big job, and it was already late, but Cam didn't care. Just then it seemed important to fix the old car. Like maybe sometime in the not-too distant future he might have a reason to use it—maybe instead of just running in circles, he might have an actual destination.

It was beyond crazy to think this way about a girl he

didn't even know, but if the thought of her could inspire him to get the GTO running again, then maybe that morning's collision wouldn't be a complete loss.

He pulled the new belt out of its package—luckily he'd bought it before Jerry and Hu's intervention—and tried to focus on the job at hand. The trouble was, he kept imagining that the car was already running, and that he was driving it: out of the garage, away from the city.

But in the vision he wasn't alone. She was there with him—her long, thick brown hair flying in the wind, because the windows were down, and the music was blaring—the playlist he'd made tonight—*her* playlist. Now it wasn't noise; it was more like the soundtrack to a life he didn't have. A life spent *with* someone—not always alone.

He wanted all of those things. It was too late and he was too tired to lie to himself.

Cam kept working through the night and into the early hours of the morning. He didn't even stop to eat—just grabbed some Cheetos from his workbench. A little motor grease mixed with fake cheese dust never hurt anyone.

It was past three when he finally got the car back together again. Then he closed his eyes and did something he never, ever allowed himself to do. He made a wish. He wished that the car would start. Cam didn't let himself wish for more than that. Not yet.

He turned the key.

And the GTO actually started. Cam let out a whoop, then jumped out and dropped the hood. He opened the garage door. Got back in the car, ready to go.

Cam slid the car into gear. And felt the engine stall. He tried again, felt it catch for a moment.

Then: nothing.

For a second there, it had almost been alive. Something had *almost* worked. Cam closed his eyes and rested his head against the steering wheel.

Hadn't he learned there was no point in making wishes? They never came true.

Cam was pedaling as fast as he could, breathing fast, legs pumping, but no matter how much he pushed, it was like his bike was standing still. It was a busy intersection, somewhere south of Houston Street, close to rush hour. The light was green, and he pedaled and pushed as hard as he could, but still the cars streamed past him, their honking horns echoing in his ears. His chest tight, he tried to take in great gulpfuls of air, but it was like the air just wouldn't reach his lungs. Night fell, and he kept pedaling, still stuck in the same spot . . . until the bike's front wheel fell off, and Cam lurched forward. He felt the back wheel fall away, and then the rest of the bike crumbled like it was made of sand. Then he started running, but soon his right foot dissolved beneath him, and he stumbled. He tried to catch himself, but his left foot was gone too, turned to dust beneath him as the rest of his body crumbled into the pavement.

He awoke, sweating, to the sound of his phone ringing. He fumbled around for it, finding it in the passenger seat beside him. Daylight streamed in from the open garage door. He looked down at his still-ringing phone: LONNIE.

"Yeah?" he answered, still confused and groggy. After that dream, his chest felt tight and his stomach felt sick.

"You coming in today or not?" Lonnie demanded.

Cam opened his mouth to make an excuse, then remembered the death of the Fantom. "No, Lonnie. Remember . . . ?"

"Well, what do you want me to do with your new bike, then?"

Cam took a deep breath of cold morning air, and stared out the windshield at the quiet street. "What new bike . . . ?" he asked slowly.

Lonnie's voice sounded irritated and harried—like always. "The one your *girlfriend* dropped off for you this morning."

Click. The line went dead. Cam stared at his phone.

It couldn't be her. But it *had* to be.

It seemed impossible: while he had been thinking about her, she had been thinking about him. And buying him a new bike.

Cam shook himself out of the remnants of the dream, vaulted out of the GTO, and sprinted for the train.

When he got off the train at the other end, he kept on running.

He was excited to see his new bike. Yeah, that was definitely it.

It wasn't like he was all that curious about his "girlfriend," the one who had apparently left it for him.

Nope, he told himself. That wasn't it at all.

THREE

Ride safe.

That's all the note said.

No digits.

But he did, in fact, have a brand-new bike—so there was that.

In a weird way, her giving him the bike was sort of a relief. It made him feel about 30 percent less stupid for casting her in the starring role of his ridiculous daydreams (complete with playlist). Because he had clearly *more* than crossed her mind as well.

Cam ran his hands over the glossy new paint, smiling at the fact that the bike was *his*.

He took off like a shot out of the front entrance of Lafayette Messenger. He flew into the stream of traffic heading across Canal—all the faces he passed were a blur again. Just the way it should be. The sun was warm on his skin and the city looked a lot less dingy and gray now that he was back up to speed.

He made his first run, but didn't hurry back to Lonnie and captivity. He rode toward the park to try out his new Sugino. It was a top-of-the line bike—a fixed gear.

Someone had done her homework. He tried to make himself stop grinning. His mom always used to say, "All things are relative." Compared to the day he'd had yesterday, today was a freaking dream come true.

Cam rode up the handrails on the steps in the park, scared some tourists, then left the park and rode as fast as he could down Broadway, weaving in and out of the sea of cars, cabs, and buses.

The day was growing hot, but he didn't feel it when he was going full speed. Cam raced back up one of the paths, into the park, where a bunch of kids practicing their moves caught his attention. All of a sudden it seemed like he was surrounded by something he'd never even noticed before—parkour. He stopped to watch. Cam knew from his web surfing that they were kong-vaulting off the big rocks at the edge of the park.

He remembered the steps he'd read about: you run toward whatever the obstacle is, dive over it with your palms flat on the surface, push off, legs up, land, then keep running and repeat with the next object in your way.

He sat transfixed, watching them practice. The city was doing some kind of construction on the old park amphitheater. The parkour kids were making use of the big piles of concrete blocks. This was as good a spot as any for lunch. He pulled out the sandwich he'd picked up on his way out of work and ate slowly, watching the kids try out some more moves. By the time he balled up his wrapper and tossed it into the trash, they'd packed it in for the day. He stood, ready to head back, but then a new kid caught his attention, jumping over a huge stack of lumber and taking off at a run, up onto the stage.

"Hey!" he called, without thinking.

It was her. Same hoodie. Same brown hair flying. It was definitely his mystery girl.

She turned, losing her balance in the process, teetering for a few seconds before recovering and rolling backward to land on her feet.

She met his eyes and they stared at each other for a few seconds.

And then she took off at a run, up the stairs and out of sight.

For the second time in two days, the girl had up and run off without a word. It was a pretty annoying habit, actually.

He didn't think, just got back on his bike and started pedaling in the direction she'd disappeared.

He'd thought he'd never see her again, but now that she'd bought him the bike—*and* he'd run into her accidentally in a city of eight million people—there was no way he was letting her go without a chase. He slid down the stone steps at the side of the park, then caught sight of her crossing the street. Cam followed. At least two cars honked at him as he wove quickly through traffic.

A long, flat truck with a mechanical arm was parked on the street. The arm was partially extended. He kept watching the girl as she jumped on some poor person's car, leapt onto the flat part of the truck, did that run-up-the-side trick (tic-tac, his brain reminded him) along the metal arm, and then vaulted into the bucket.

He slid to a stop at the base of the truck.

She'd cornered herself, for some reason.

She pulled her headphones out, carefully. He watched her wrap them in a loop and stash them in a zippered pocket on the side of her sweatshirt. Cam had noticed they were Beats—nice ones. Between the quality earbuds and the brand-new Sugino she'd bought for a stranger, she definitely had access to money.

"What do you want?" she demanded, leaning over the side to peer down at him.

Standing there, looking up at her, Cam was struck by the sudden, absurd thought that she was like Juliet standing on her balcony, as pretty as the sun, or whatever poetic business his ninth-grade English teacher had tried to drill into him.

Cam forced his brain to focus. He didn't know exactly what to say to the girl in the bucket, so he went with a version of the truth. "Thanks. For the bike."

She looked down at him, warily—like he'd been the one to chase her up there or something. "You're welcome." Her voice was clipped, as though the words were hard to say.

She seemed very wary of him. On second thought, definitely not very Juliet-like.

"Where'd you learn to do parkour?" he asked her.

Hoodie girl rolled her eyes.

"What, didn't I say it right?"

"I gotta go."

Cam raised his eyebrows. "Yeah, clearly you're in a

gigantic hurry. That's a real fast lane you've chosen up there." When she didn't answer, he pressed on. "What's your name?"

She looked away, biting her lip. It seemed like there were a lot of things she didn't want to say. Apparently even her name fell into that category.

"You ride?" Cam asked her, figuring he'd distract her with some misdirection.

She sniffed like he'd offended her. "That bike's a ball and chain."

"Yeah, well . . . anybody can climb a tree," Cam shot back.

She smiled, though for some reason it seemed involuntary. "I'd like to see that."

It wasn't much of an opening. But he figured, what the hell?

It was easy enough to climb up onto the truck. Then he started to scale the metal arm. She'd scrambled up in a matter of seconds, but Cam was treating it more like a balance beam—moving slowly, trying not to lose his footing. The angle of the metal arm was a lot steeper than it had looked from the ground. Or maybe she'd just made it look much too easy.

He was maybe six feet away from the bucket, but he was starting to lose his footing. Moving slow wasn't going to get him up into the bucket where she stood.

"Maybe you should stick to the bike," she told him. But her voice had lost that clipped tone. She was almost smiling.

Cam shot her another look. Okay, that cinched it.

"Screw it." He took the last few steps at a run and jumped into the bucket, landing beside her.

They stood face-to-face.

"I'm Cam," he said, with the little bit of breath he had left. They were so close, their bodies were almost touching.

"Nikki . . ."

Nikki. This close, she was even more . . . *more* than he'd realized the day before. Her skin was pale, but she had a light smattering of freckles across the bridge of her nose. You'd have to be close up to even see them. Her lips were full . . . Cam had to force himself to stop staring at them. He could hear her breathing. The strange hold she'd had over his thoughts the last twenty-four hours was nothing compared to the effect of standing so close to her. He heard her breath catch.

"Show me something else," he said, his voice low.

Nikki was staring at him. Maybe considering.

And then, without a word, she hopped up onto the edge of the bucket and jumped.

Cam forgot to breathe for a few seconds, stepping to

the edge and looking down to see her land on the stairs of a nearby parking garage. She took off at a run—up the stairs.

The roof was her destination. Cam looked down. It hadn't been easy getting up here. Getting down would be worse, but it'd be over much faster. He held his breath and jumped.

He was already pretty sure he'd follow her anywhere.

And . . . wipeout.

It wasn't the first time chasing a girl had landed him flat on his back with the wind knocked out of him. Hell, it wasn't the first time *this* girl had landed him flat on his back. He had the sneaking suspicion (hope? fear?) that it wouldn't be the last.

Cam had survived the jump over to the street just fine, and he'd even managed to make it up the stairs. But once they were on the roof of the parking garage, Nikki had vaulted over a car and glanced back at him with a look that clearly dared him to follow.

So he'd taken a deep breath, run as fast as he could, launched himself over the first car, and . . . wipeout.

He'd also managed to set off the car's alarm.

A feeling of shame washed over him. Cam was used to being the best. At work, he was the fastest rider, without question. When he was learning martial arts as a kid, he'd been the quickest to pick up every move in class; it didn't matter if it was karate or Muay Thai.

But he'd just gotten schooled in parkour. By a girl.

Nikki stood over him. *Way* over him—she was peering down from the roof of an SUV.

She frowned, but there didn't seem to be much sympathy in her look. It was the same frown his eighth-grade teacher used to shoot his way—disappointment with just a hint of you-are-an-idiot mixed in.

"If you want to do parkour, you have to learn how to *see*," she told him, vaulting down like she had cat DNA. She pulled something small and black out of her pocket and held it up; the alarm beeped twice and then was silent.

"I can see fine," Cam ground out, as he heaved himself to his feet and started picking the gravel bits out of his palms. "How'd you shut off that alarm?"

Nikki shrugged. "Little gift from a friend. Comes in handy sometimes." She went on in a serious tone: "Look, I know these moves look easy, and it does take guts, but it's more important to slow down and think about what you're doing. Otherwise, you're gonna get hurt. So, first tip: if you want to vault the car, don't look at the *car*. Look at where the car *isn't*."

Cam fought the urge to call her Yoda—because Yoda was *not* sexy. He nodded and watched her clear a big black Mercedes SL like she was stepping over a puddle.

Cam tried the same car, concentrating on where the car *wasn't*.

He cleared it. She met his grin with one of her own, then ran and jumped.

And disappeared.

She vanished right through a gap in the floor.

Cam rushed forward, peering over the edge.

It was a straight drop down to the next level. That took guts all right. Or maybe Nikki wasn't as good at this as she'd seemed. He couldn't see her anywhere. He raced frantically to the stairs, taking them five, six at a time, sliding down, assuming the worst.

But halfway down, he spotted her standing there, totally fine—she wasn't even out of breath.

"How'd you . . . ?" He gaped.

She smiled at him. "It was nice to meet you, Cam. Take care."

What? She was leaving? What the hell was wrong with this girl?

Also, what the hell was wrong with him that he seemed to care so freaking much?

Stunned, Cam stared at her retreating figure, then whirled around as he heard someone speak.

"Who are you?"

Cam whipped his head around, trying to find the owner of the voice—a male voice. He caught sight of three guys across the gap from Nikki.

"What are you doing here, Dylan?" she called across to them.

"Just keeping an eye on you, Niks," one of them answered.

"You been spying on me the whole time?" Nikki sounded annoyed.

"You working out alone?" the guy countered.

"So what?" Cam saw Nikki's chin lift. But her eyes didn't match her defiant stance.

"Gotta be careful," the guy told her. His tone sounded sort of paternal, which seemed weird to Cam.

One of the other guys—the tallest one—took a step forward. "Who is this guy?"

"He's nobody," Nikki said quickly.

Thanks a lot. Cam glared at her, but she didn't seem to notice.

The third guy spoke up. "Haven't seen you around before." His chest was all puffed out like he was going to challenge Cam to a duel or something. Reminded him of Hu, only smaller, and also less Chinese.

"Haven't been around," Cam said lightly, not rising to the bait.

"Where'd you find him?" the guy she'd called Dylan asked, turning to Nikki.

Him. The guy managed to inject that one syllable with a boatload of condescension.

"He found me."

Well, that's not exactly true, Cam thought.

"You following her?" Now this Dylan guy was getting all puffed up.

Cam kept his voice level. "I saw her in the park."

Dylan stared Cam down. "Yeah, well, lesson's over. This is dangerous stuff. You can get hurt real bad if you don't know what you're doing."

It was really nice how concerned all these strangers seemed to be about his physical safety. Cam resisted the urge to tell him that, based on his extensive web research, he already knew all about the danger to his Achilles tendon.

"Let's bounce," Dylan said.

Cam took a step forward, maybe to follow, maybe to protest—but he never got to figure out which one.

The parking structure's elevator was moving up from below. But these guys didn't wait for it to get there.

They all followed Dylan through a gap in the floor, landing right on *top* of the elevator. Cam watched them disappear, heading up.

Nikki was the last to step off when the main compartment reached the next floor. Cam stared in disbelief as his mystery girl disappeared through the ceiling.

She was gone. Again.

When he got back to the cherry picker, Cam realized what he'd forgotten to do in his rush to chase after her.

He hadn't locked his bike. The lock lay on the ground, but the new bike was history.

Cam sat down on the curb.

He sat still for a long time, thinking about everything he'd found that day—everything that was now gone.

To be honest, he wasn't thinking all that much about the bike. Which was the stupidest part of all.

Since his own carelessness had cost him his new bike before he'd managed even a full day of runs, Cam knew he was down to his last couple of options.

Angie's neighbor Karl had made it pretty clear he was

interested in Cam's tools, so on his way back home Cam left a message with the guy's wife.

Karl showed up at dusk and asked to take a look. "Thought you weren't keen on selling," he said, in his deliberate way. He pawed through the tools, even though he'd already seen them all. He was probably making sure they were all there.

"Yeah, well, circumstances changed," Cam told him. "Price is six."

"Sorry about that. Your circumstances, I mean. Well, you know I want 'em. But my wife won't let me go over four."

Cam sighed. "My rent is five-fifty."

Karl met his eyes. He nodded slowly. "Deal."

As Karl counted out the money in twenties, he looked over at the GTO. "So about those circumstances of yours . . . you any closer to selling her?"

Cam felt his jaw tighten and he shook his head. "I told you—it was my dad's. I'm gonna have to hold on to it."

Karl bent to pick up Cam's—now *his*—tools. "Too bad. Nice car. Well, you know where to find me," Karl told him, and walked back out of the garage.

Cam watched Karl's retreating figure disappear. He looked back over at the GTO, thinking how stupid it was that he was even keeping it—now that he no longer even had the tools to fix it.

For some reason he just couldn't let go. Cam walked outside and sat down on the edge of the sidewalk as darkness fell over the neighborhood. People came home from work and disappeared into houses. He could smell various suppers being cooked up and down the block.

People with families lived here, mostly. Like he used to have.

Cam closed his eyes, remembering. There had been a time when things were good. Before his dad got sent up. Before his mom got sick. He remembered, once, his dad taking him for a drive, all the way out to Coney Island. They'd stopped for ices, and sat on a bench overlooking the water, and his dad had talked to him, almost like Cam was all grown up. His father had talked about his dreams—how he planned to take Cam and his mother away. How one day they'd pack up the GTO and drive all day and night, and land in a new place, one where things would be better.

That drive was the closest they ever got to a road trip.

Instead, a few weeks later, his dad pulled a robbery not five blocks from their apartment, and when the clerk didn't cooperate, his father shot him.

Cam had pictured that last job his dad pulled so many times, he almost believed he'd actually been there. He could see the too-bright fluorescent lights of the store reflected in everyone's faces, washing them out, making them look sick. He imagined the way the old clerk's hands must have shaken as he opened the cash drawer. Maybe that tremor was what allowed his father to notice when the clerk tried to hit the silent alarm. Cam closed his eyes, imagining the fear blooming in the clerk's chest as he realized Cam's father had just pulled the trigger. The fear and terror of the poor guy's final moments of life. The blood.

Cam had often wondered why, when he imagined the scene, it was never from his father's point of view. Instead, he always thought of that poor old guy who'd probably just been trying to keep his job. He opened his eyes. It was full dark now; everyone was home. The houses were shut up tight.

By the time he stood up, his legs were stiff and his head ached. He walked inside the garage, alone.

Alone, like always. He'd let himself daydream about a girl he didn't even know, and he knew now that it had been a mistake. A guy like him, with no luck, was never going to find her for a third time.

He couldn't shake the feeling that maybe she'd crashed

into his life for a reason, though—other than reminding him how freaking lonely he was.

Maybe it had been so he could learn about parkour. So he could have something to fill up the miserable empty hours not spent at work or sleeping.

Cam stayed up late, watching videos on his phone, visiting the parkour artists' forums—that was one thing he'd learned, that a lot of people said it was an art, not a sport. He also learned the names of more of the moves; he read about the history of the movement.

No matter what he saw and read, Cam kept thinking: *I could do that.* He'd spent countless hours learning and practicing karate when he was younger, and he'd started getting into jujitsu when his mom got sick. He had to give up lessons—too expensive. And if you weren't a student, you couldn't use the gym. But in parkour, the city was your gym. It was perfect.

When his phone was almost out of juice, Cam plugged it into the charger and lay down. He drifted off to sleep, excited about tomorrow for a change.

FOUR

THE NEXT MORNING, Cam discovered that parkour was nowhere near as easy as Nikki and the others had made it look.

For the first couple of days, Cam kept telling himself he'd get better, and thinking about his friend Ryan from middle school. Ryan had shown up on the subway one day toting a long, battered black case. The two of them usually rode to school together. Usually, neither of them carried much of anything on the train. They both got the government-sponsored free "lunch." (Technically it was food, but Cam always thought it seemed kind of charitable to call it *lunch*.) Neither of them ever carried too many books home. But that day, there was Ryan with this huge case. His friend told him glumly that his mother was making him learn the trombone.

Cam had laughed at him. Even by seventh grade, he'd learned to laugh at anyone who tried too hard at anything school related.

But even though Ryan used to laugh *with* him at people who actually tried, he *had* learned to play that trombone. Cam went over to his place after school sometimes when his mom worked late. There was always snack food in Ryan's kitchen. But the downside, post-trombone, was that Ryan had started obsessively practicing. At first, it sounded like someone was torturing a cat.

Then one day, a couple of years later, Cam was in ninth or tenth grade, sitting bored in an assembly, and Ryan had stood up with a couple of other band guys. He and Ryan had drifted apart and stopped hanging out after they started high school. Cam hadn't heard him torture that trombone in years. The performance started with a solo from Ryan, and Cam sat up in shock, listening—the sound coming out of that instrument was now definitely *music*. He'd been so surprised he'd nearly fallen out of his chair. Cam even hung around after the assembly and told Ryan he'd done a nice job. His old friend had looked very surprised, but pleased.

As Cam took his first painful stabs at parkour, he thought about Ryan. About how his friend obsessively practiced, even when he sounded like utter garbage. He'd kept at it, until all the notes flowed together and sounded like music. And that was what Cam vowed he was going to do.

He started small—focusing on tic-tacs off the wall outside Lafayette Messenger. He kept pushing for more height, and sometimes he wiped out.

At a low point, lying on the ground with pieces of asphalt digging into his back, both his knees scraped all to hell, Cam reflected that at least the trombone didn't cause physical injury. But still he kept at it.

He took the subway uptown to a strip of Riverside Park that was always empty. For a small section of the park, the benches were lined up perfectly for him to leap from one to the next. He only bit it once, tasting the metal of the bench, giving himself a fat lip that lasted for two days. As he kept practicing, his body started to hurt less. His movements started to flow.

Instead of being just a bunch of awkward, unrelated moves, everything started to connect.

Almost like music.

The scraped palms and knees, the fat lip, the aching

muscles—all of it was worth it. Because even though the girl was gone, and the bike was gone, there was still the city. And now he could see it clearly for what it actually was.

A gigantic playground.

Parkour, tracing, whatever you wanted to call it, was perfect for him, because it required nothing: no companions, no gear, just muscles and nerves. And a complete ability to, as Angie put it, "jump around like somebody with no health insurance shouldn't even *think* of doing." When Cam started jumping off the roof of the garage and practicing wall tricks on the side of her house, Angie would hustle Joey inside before he got any ideas.

Lonnie, the prince of Lafayette Messenger Service, had rescued Cam from his bikeless state with a garbage loaner bike. It might have felt like charity—except that Cam knew he was Lonnie's fastest rider, so it wasn't a completely selfless act. At least Lonnie didn't give him too much crap about losing *two* bikes in a week.

Even with the loaner bike, Cam was racing through his deliveries faster than usual, so he could get back to practicing his moves. When he looked around the city now, he saw everything with new eyes. Every object could be used to give him momentum as he practiced: vaulting, leaping, sprinting. He still lost his footing occasionally, and had a few falls. But every day he got stronger, more precise.

He started showing up at Washington Square Park too, working out with the kids who trained there. It wasn't an official jam—a meet-up of tracers—but he saw the same people every day, started learning a few new tricks.

For six days, he spent every spare moment practicing. On Sunday, he had the whole day free to train, and he spent most of it at the park. By the time dusk rolled around, Cam had already put in a long day, but he kept at it. Everyone else had probably gone home to eat dinner, but Cam kept vaulting over the high stone railing at the edge of the park, over and down, then sprinting back up again. When he finally nailed a perfect landing, he grinned and sat down on the steps, replaying the jump in his mind. Except in the imaginary version, *she* was there watching him. Acting impressed. Maybe showing some appreciation for his new skills . . .

A motorcycle revved, catching Cam's attention. The rider was stopped, pulled over at the edge of the park, his features indistinct, silhouetted with the setting sun behind him.

The guy was watching him, though. Cam could feel it. There was something about him—something familiar. The stranger had noticed that Cam was looking at him; that much was clear. But he held his ground for another full minute before revving the bike again and tearing away.

The next day at work, Cam pedaled so fast he thought the loaner might not make it through the day; he wanted to get through with the boring stuff because he had a destination. As soon as he delivered his last package, Cam was planning to return to the parking garage where Nikki had led him.

It was a good place to train. And, of course, there was a chance she might show up again. That would qualify as a bonus.

When the workday was finally done, Cam rode the loaner out to the garage. He locked it up against a concrete pillar, then took off running, psyching himself up for the jump, his muscles humming, his mind clear. The mantra Nikki had taught him echoed in his head. He wasn't looking at the line of cars, he was looking beyond them—where the cars *weren't*—to the empty space where he would land. He pushed off hard, held his breath. And vaulted clear over the cars. The only sound was his breathing. No alarms. He'd cleared it, just like she had.

Feeling a rush of something like joy, he kept running, didn't slow down . . . and failed to see the gap between the levels. For a few seconds he was flying—though headed down, not up. He tensed his muscles, then relaxed, timing it all exactly right; again, he stuck the landing. Cam was grinning, his adrenaline pumping. He heard the word "nice" escape his lips, even though no one was around to appreciate what he'd just pulled off. He hopped on top of the elevator car, remembering Dylan's trick, but then he heard a voice.

"Somebody's been practicing."

Cam let out an undignified squeak. Sure, he could jump over a line of cars, down two levels, and stick the landing, but Dylan saying three words, *that* turned him into a freaking mouse.

Dylan was standing on the same level, on the other side of the garage. If he had heard the mouse squeak, he didn't show it. He called over to Cam: "You should come work out with us."

Cam stared at him. *Us.* As in a group of people that included Nikki.

"I never see you guys around," he told Dylan, keeping his voice casual (and squeak free).

Of course, it was completely *not* for lack of trying that he hadn't seen them, but he wasn't going to volunteer that information.

Dylan shrugged. "We're a tight group. Like to keep to ourselves."

Cam waited for him to continue, pretending he didn't care whether or not he got the invite to train with them. He forced a shrug, but fake shrugging turned out to be more of a physical challenge than the two-story drop. Cam thought he saw Dylan smile—maybe he'd noticed the awkward hunch-back moment—but his next words were a relief.

"Loujaine floating terminal—in Brooklyn. You know it?"

Cam nodded, tried hard not to grin. Then he realized he actually *didn't* know the place. "No! I . . ." Just then, the eleva-tor started moving downward.

Dylan called down to him: "Gowanus Bay. Pier Twenty-One. See you tomorrow at dawn."

Dawn took pretty much forever to arrive. Sleep was not happening. Part of the problem: he was afraid that if he did drift off, he might *over*sleep. He'd been known to sleep right through his alarm on more than one occasion. He knew if he blew off Dylan's invite to train, he probably wouldn't get another. So he lay with his phone right under his pillow, and checked it every half hour or so.

The other reason he was wide-awake at three in the

morning: stupidity. He would have felt embarrassed if anyone else knew just how excited he was to see Nikki again—to show her how much better he'd gotten. Cam knew she'd be impressed.

Or at least he *hoped* she'd be impressed.

The problem was, he'd pictured himself showing off his newfound skills for her so many times in his head, it had started to seem impossible that it would actually happen.

In Cam's experience, imagining something good equaled "never gonna happen."

He tossed and turned, dozing off and then hurtling awake again because he was tracing in his dreams. He kept waking up mid-fall, breathing hard.

Cam fell asleep for real just before dawn. He dreamed about Nikki.

This time they were at the beach—but not a dirty, sad strip of land like the beaches Cam had seen around New York. They were standing on some faraway shore with clean white sand glimmering in the sun. In the sunlight, Nikki's eyes were the color of the sky.

His alarm ripped him back to reality. He had turned the phone up to maximum volume, and set it on the most obnoxious sound possible. Cam fumbled for the phone in the dark, knocking it onto the floor. He swore, rolled out of bed, picked up the phone, grabbed his sweatshirt, and was out the door.

For the whole long subway ride, Cam couldn't sit still. The train was nearly empty, but an older woman sat beside him, glaring in annoyance at his bouncing leg before moving away from him. Cam ignored her. When he finally reached Pier 21, he forced himself to slow down from a sprint to a jog. He spotted the group waiting for him in front of an old chain-link fence.

"Hey," he said.

Nikki's eyes were on the pavement, her hood pulled over her head. Cam forced himself to focus on Dylan. Because Cam was being Mr. Casual.

Dylan gave him a nod. "This is Tate, and Jax."

Tate shook his hand, but Jax gave him a grin and offered a fist bump.

"Cam."

"Oh, we know," Jax told him, grinning.

"How's it going?" Tate said.

"And that's my sister, Nikki," Dylan told Cam.

Her head shot up. "We've already met," she spit out. She turned on her heel, grabbing the chain-link fence and scrambling up the side. She then flipped over the fence and ran out of sight.

"Okay . . ." Cam stared after her.

"Show-off." Jax nodded toward Nikki's retreating figure.

Dylan rolled his eyes, slid the gate open, and the rest of them *walked* through.

So she really had been showing off.

The ship was massive—it must have been a cargo ship once. But now, abandoned, it was just another part of the jungle gym. An awesome part, filled with jumps and obstacles (the good kind—not people, who mostly just got in the way). On the ship, it was just the five of them. The boys caught up to Nikki and stood in a circle.

"So should I . . . ?" Cam looked at the others.

"Just try and keep up," Nikki told him, taking off fast again, vaulting and jumping from one level to the next without a pause. He grinned and took off after her.

Cam counted five decks on the massive ship. The metal had once been painted white, but was now rusted through in most places. They began making their way up from the bottom level, but when they doubled back and dropped down, using the railing for leverage, Cam was surprised to find his landing cushioned by a pile of old mattresses.

He was keeping up, Cam told himself as he ran, and it was mostly true. He wasn't as graceful as the others, but, then again, this boat was *theirs*. It wasn't until they all made a steep jump from a narrow perch on one side of the deck that Cam went down, hard.

The others kept running, but one of the figures stopped, then turned back to wait for him. Maybe to check on him?

It was Nikki.

He pulled himself to his feet, and jogged to catch up to her, breathing hard. For a few seconds they were face-to-face, just like that day in the cherry picker. She seemed to be trying to figure something out—but what? Whether or not he was okay? Whether or not she was sorry she'd gone back for him?

Whether or not she thought he was the most annoying person on the planet?

"You're not careful," she observed. A crease had appeared in her forehead. She was letting her guard down, just a little, after seeming so standoffish in front of her brother and the others.

Cam felt confused—*he* wasn't careful? "*You* were the one who smashed into *me* after jumping off a five-story building," he told her.

She bit her lip—which seemed to be a habit of hers. "Yeah. But it took me a long time to learn how to do that. Besides, that was an unusual day. I don't usually stop traffic. Or wreck out bike messengers. I'm careful. I swear. You have to swear you will be too, yeah?"

She didn't wait for his promise, just turned without another word and chased off after the others.

Cam shook his head. He seriously doubted that being *careful* would get him very far with this crowd. He stood up, feeling defiant, and pushed himself to catch up to the group. He got back into the rhythm of things, copying Nikki's moves now. Trying to keep up with *her*—pushing himself to best her.

He followed as they vaulted up from one level to the next until they were on the uppermost deck. Too late, Cam saw that the metal of the deck beneath his feet was *moving*. The grate was designed to slide open to allow access to the cargo hold below. But, high on adrenaline, and not knowing the ship as well as the others, who all stopped short of the gap, Cam leapt across.

Well, he tried to leap across. What actually happened was that he didn't get enough height in his jump, a fact he became aware of halfway across the gap, when his arms and legs started flailing around like he was swimming in midair. He missed the far edge of the gap, but managed at the last second to grab on to a length of chain that hung from the metal ledge.

He dangled in midair, holding on for dear life.

"Seriously?!" he heard one of them—maybe Jax—yell.

"He's probably dead." That was Dylan.

Cam made the mistake of looking down. Five *stories* down into the empty bowels of the ship. He took a deep breath and tried to pull himself up, but his arms were fully extended and there was nothing but air for his feet to hold on to. He forced himself to stop kicking. It wasn't doing any good.

A pair of boots landed with a thud just above his head. Cam looked up, but the sun was behind the figure and he couldn't see the face clearly. Whoever it was had just made the same jump he'd missed like it was nothing.

The guy hunched down on his knees, and Cam got his first look at his face: he was older, maybe thirty or more, dark hair, slim, but there was something familiar about him.

"Hey. You must be Cam."

Cam stared incredulously at the man, then nodded and grunted, "Yeah."

The guy smiled, taking his time, while Cam struggled to hold on. "Dylan told me about you. Said you're new to parkour. Said you're pretty good." He paused, and smiled down at Cam. "Clearly a few kinks to work out, though."

"Yeah," Cam said again, through closed teeth.

Pull me up or just go away and leave me alone to die, he was thinking. But by this point he had a feeling Nikki was watching, so he kept trying to remain cool while slipping and preparing to fall.

The guy went for Option A, and in one quick motion grabbed Cam by the arms and pulled him up onto the deck. Cam lay there heaving for breath like a dying fish.

So much for the cool factor.

Cam closed his eyes again.

"I'm Miller."

Cam forced himself to raise his eyelids, then took the hand the new guy was offering him. He let Miller pull him to his feet.

"Thanks."

"Pick a fight with gravity before you're ready, you can expect a beatdown."

Thanks for the excellent advice.

"Thought I could make it," Cam said aloud.

"Stop thinking," Miller corrected. "Stay in the moment."

"I still don't really know what I'm doing," he admitted in a low voice, shaking his head, feeling discouraged. He looked up and saw Nikki. She hadn't made the leap across. Apparently it didn't take all that long to simply walk *around* the gap.

Miller surprised him with a friendly smile and a pat on the back. "But that's the great thing about parkour, my friend. There are no rules."

The others had followed Nikki, and they stepped forward, forming a semicircle around Cam. "You okay?" Dylan asked.

"I'm good," Cam answered.

"Oh my God, dude. That was ninety-eight percent pure psycho." Jax was looking at him with either admiration or pity—Cam couldn't tell which.

"What was the other two percent?" Nikki asked dryly.

"Luck," Dylan answered. "Definitely luck."

Cam snorted. His name and the word *luck* did not belong in the same sentence, unless the word *bad* was added in there too.

"Well, what would you call it?" Dylan asked him. "Seeing as how you're alive and all."

Cam shrugged. "I was just trying to keep up."

Nikki shot him an angry look, but she was visibly upset. Her eyes were suspiciously bright.

He'd managed to throw her words back at her—*and* make her feel bad by almost dying.

Definitely worth it.

FIVE

THE BENEFITS of almost dying continued. Cam had earned a ticket to the gang's lair, a space deep in the bowels of the cargo ship, all rigged out for postjam hanging: old TV, Xbox, Ping-Pong table. Miller had apparently brought lunch too, because the table was piled high with Wendy's bags.

"Sit," Dylan told him. "You've earned it."

"Cam?" Jax looked at Cam from across the table. "What's that short for? Camaro?"

Tate pinged Jax in the head with a ketchup packet. "Seriously, dude?" He turned to Cam. "Ignore him."

"It's Cameron," he answered, smiling. "But I wish it were Camaro."

"Where you from?" Dylan asked, taking a big bite of burger.

"Queens."

"City native, huh?" Dylan said.

Cam nodded. He noticed Miller regarding him steadily from across the table.

"Wherever you're from, you're a natural, dude," Jax said. "I mean at parkour."

Cam smiled at him again. He seemed like a good dude. The kind of guy it was hard to be in a bad mood around. He'd been hanging around wannabe-hipster bike messengers and mid-level Chinese mobsters so long he'd started to forget that it didn't always suck to hang out with other people.

Tate broke in: "You play any sports in school?"

"Barely went to high school," Cam told him. "Tried base-ball . . . once. Used to do some martial arts."

"I wasn't much of a jock in high school either," Jax told him.

Tate snorted. "Yeah. Look at you." Jax just kept eating; he seemed pretty good at ignoring Tate.

Miller broke his silence with his own question: "Where'd you do your time?"

He didn't know how Miller had figured it out. He hadn't

told any of the others. Thrown, he took a deep breath before answering. He didn't dare look across the table just then. Some girls were impressed when guys had done time. He had the feeling Nikki might not be one of them.

He shifted uncomfortably in his seat. "It's okay," Miller told him. "You're not the only one here with a record."

Cam looked around the table, wondering who the older man was referring to. He avoided Nikki's gaze. "Abbott House. Hillside."

"That's juvie," Miller observed.

"Yeah. Did six months in Otisville a couple years ago."

"What for?" Miller asked. Cam wondered if he was imagining that Miller seemed oddly invested in his answers.

Cam kept his voice level as he recited his rap sheet. "B and E. Boosting cars."

Following in his old man's illustrious footsteps.

"You ever go in hard? Pull any holdups?"

Cam stared at Miller for a moment. Speaking of his old man's footsteps. "No," Cam answered, and heard the hardness in his voice. "I didn't want to go that way."

"What do you do for money?" This was turning into Twenty Questions with Miller.

Clearly, Cam was expected to play along. It was true what his mom used to say: no such thing as a free lunch.

"I'm a bike messenger," Cam answered.

"What do you guys deliver?"

"I don't know. Business stuff . . . documents."

"At least that's what they tell you," Miller said.

Cam looked at him. It was a strange comment. Nikki caught his eye across the table—like she was trying to tell him something. She'd made a sort of sculpture out of her straw and plastic fork and knife, but she wasn't actually eating.

Cam returned Miller's gaze. "They hand me a package, I drop it off. Simple as that."

"But it could be anything, right?"

"I guess," Cam answered warily.

"You *never* look inside the bag?"

"No."

"Never?"

"No. Why would I . . . ?" Cam looked over at Nikki again.

"Curiosity," Miller suggested.

"It's none of my business."

"But you're the one carrying the package."

Cam paused, taking a drink of his soda. He raised his eyes and met Miller's gaze. "Look. As long as they pay me my money after I drop it off, I don't really care *what's* inside the bag."

Nikki let out a breath like she'd been holding it awhile,

and stabbed at her plastic sculpture with another straw. It crumbled and she continued to stare at Cam.

Miller nodded at him from across the table, smiling a little.

Cam realized it was time for the million-dollar question. "So . . . what do you guys do?"

Miller's smile widened. "We do whatever we can not to get caught." He stood, crumpling the paper his burger had come in and throwing it into the pile at the center of the table. He nodded at Cam. "Come with me."

Cam followed Miller up a set of metal stairs to a window that looked out over the back of the ship. A question flitted through his mind: Did Miller own the ship? The setup down in the hold seemed designed to look like a squat, but as Dylan had observed, Cam was a city native. He knew that city real estate didn't stay abandoned for long.

"You're a smart kid, Cam." Miller's voice broke into his thoughts. "I can tell."

"Yeah, my teachers *definitely* thought so," Cam quipped.

Miller barked a laugh. "What do they know? No money in what *they* do."

Cam smiled back. It was nice to not be judged for all his failures, for a change. They stood looking out over the water in silence for a few minutes.

Miller asked him some more questions about his life—but didn't offer anything about himself in return. Eventually, Cam noticed that the others had resumed their training on the deck; apparently they had digested their lunch. He looked down and watched Dylan and Nikki perform two flips, side by side, in almost perfect synchronicity.

"Looks like fun," Cam observed.

Miller nodded. "That's the right attitude. No limits, my friend. Only plateaus."

"Plateaus?"

"You've got to constantly push past what you think you can do, or you stay stuck."

"I like that. What else you got?"

"How about this? Parkour, free running, tracing, whatever you call it—it's really a state of mind. The real obstacles are not out there." Miller nodded toward the ship's deck. "They're in your head."

Cam followed Miller's gaze down, watching Tate clear a wide jump, barely sticking the landing. Nikki stopped to check on him. "I don't know. Those obstacles look pretty real to me."

The thing was, Cam wasn't really talking about the ship.

"Well, you're gonna have to start seeing them differently."

He watched Nikki execute a nice wall trick. "Look where the car isn't," he said aloud, remembering his first parkour lesson.

"Exactly."

Miller gave him an approving nod and moved away from the window, but Cam stayed where he was for a long time, watching Nikki.

"How's that new bike treating you?" Nikki asked as they filed through the shipyard gate.

Cam felt the blood drain from his face at her question. "Awesome!" he said, too brightly. "Thanks again. For the bike, I mean."

Nikki stared at him, a smile peeking through her frown. "You're welcome. Where is it? The bike, I mean," she said, echoing his words with a smirk.

"Oh! I left it at home today."

Her arm brushed his as they walked side by side. "Liar."

He sighed. "Somebody clipped it. I didn't want to say anything . . ."

Nikki nodded. "It's okay. I get it. You're one of those people."

"Who are *those* people?"

"The ones who can't hang on to anything nice."

Cam looked into those eyes of hers, trying, as always, not to think about everything she made him want.

"Guess I haven't had enough practice," he told her.

The moment stretched out as his words hung in the air between them. But she broke the silence first. "Probably just as well. I knew it was a bad idea. Next time I'll just take my wallet and burn it." Nikki smiled like she was trying to make it a joke, but the plan seemed to backfire. Her smile didn't reach her eyes, which were filled with something else. Pain, maybe?

"You did say that a bike was a ball and chain," Cam told her, trying to lighten the mood again. "And thanks to some crazy chick jumping on top of me, I got to find out about parkour. No bike needed for that."

"You're really getting good," she said. "Been practicing a little, huh?"

He barked a laugh. "Try constantly."

"I could have guessed you'd love it," Nikki observed. "You seem like someone who just leaps without worrying about where you'll land. Miller says I'll never be great at it because I *always* worry."

"You seem pretty great to me." Her eyes widened. "At parkour," he added quickly.

"I've hit one of Miller's plateaus, probably."

"Come on, Niks!" Dylan's voice called out. Nikki looked relieved as she jogged to catch up with the others.

Cam followed, stopping her with a hand on her arm. "So . . . you guys all work together, right? With Miller?"

Cam could see that she knew what he was asking, but she didn't answer his question. She pulled away from him. "See you around, Cam."

Her evasiveness confirmed his suspicions. Miller was their boss, that much was clear. And it was also pretty clear that they weren't supposed to talk about whatever they were into with him.

Cam watched her join the others. Miller was standing beside his motorcycle, and the recognition clicked into place like a switch being flipped.

Miller was the guy who'd been watching him work out at the park. He gave Cam a nod, like he knew Cam had recognized him. "Nice to meet you, Cam," Miller called. "Listen, don't let these guys get you into trouble." He put on his helmet, started his bike, and rode away.

Before Cam could catch up to the other four, they'd grabbed on to the back of a flat trailer carrying a monster truck. Nikki was holding on to one of the huge wheels. She looked back at Cam as the trailer drove out of sight.

She was always gone so fast. He never had time to figure her out.

At the thought of the word *time,* his stomach dropped.

He'd missed his appointment to settle up with Jerry.

Cam raced to the subway, cursing steadily under his breath as he waited for the train. When he reached Chinatown, he ran flat out all the way to the fish store. He flew in the door, but the little old woman who always stood in the back didn't flinch; she just continued breaking a brick of fish food into tiny pieces, then carefully sprinkling the food into the aquarium beside her. She glanced up lazily at Cam's entrance, but didn't stop what she was doing.

A man holding a small net came out of the back of the shop. "Where's Jerry?" Cam asked him, breathless.

"You just missed him."

"Well, do you know when he'll be back?"

"When he returns."

Cam let out a grunt of frustration at the unhelpful answer, then ran back out the door. The trip home seemed to take even longer than usual, and again Cam arrived too late. He watched his car being "repossessed" by a tow truck driven by Mr. Personality, Hu.

He felt sick, seeing his GTO being carted away.

"Hey, stop!" he yelled, running alongside the moving tow truck.

"Cam, you didn't tell me you had such a sweet ride," Jerry said through the passenger window.

Cam reached into his pocket and pulled out his cash— holding up the wad of bills and thrusting them through the truck window. Jerry reached out and grabbed the cash, but Hu didn't stop the truck.

"We're knocking five grand off your tab, in exchange for the car. You've got a month to get us the rest. Don't look so sad, Cam. You clear your debt, I'll give her back to you."

He did the math in his head. With interest, he'd still owe over twelve thousand. "How am I supposed to find that much in one month?"

"Not my problem." Jerry shook his head, then frowned, reaching a hand up to pat his hair back into place.

The truck started to pull away, and Cam tried to hold on. "Jerry, cut me some slack . . ."

Hu hit the brakes, and Jerry opened the door Cam had been holding on to; Cam nearly tripped. Jerry hopped out of the truck and got in his face—which was usually Hu's job. "You still don't understand how this works, do you?" Jerry took another half step forward, and added in a lower voice,

"If you don't pay, we don't shoot *you*." Jerry had really lost his cool. His hair was a complete mess.

Cam caught Angie's movement out of the corner of his eye. Her place was a few houses down—she was taking out the garbage. Cam met Jerry's gaze and understood.

A cold feeling went through him. He thought about Angie, and Joey.

And then he thought about Nikki.

Finding that much money in one month was impossible. Which meant that seeing her again was impossible too. Unless he could make a lot of money, fast.

He looked up and realized that Hu and Jerry had towed his father's car away. He trudged back to Angie's, but he only got halfway up the drive.

Angie met him there, her face a mask of anger. His two plastic crates were sitting next to her, containing all of his worldly possessions. He saw Joey open the screen door, but his mother barked at him to go inside.

"Angie, I'm sorry . . ." he began, but he didn't know how to finish the sentence.

He didn't have to figure it out, because Angie slapped him, hard. "Your *friends* gave Joey a ride home from school today, Cam." Her voice shook. "Those . . . *thugs* brought my son home from school!" A tear escaped from the corner of her eye, and she swiped it away.

"Angie, I . . ." Cam felt helpless, and sick. Seeing Angie so scared and angry was like letting his mom down all over again.

"I don't want to see you anywhere around me or my son or this house ever again. Do you hear me? Stay away from us, Cam! I mean it." She threw both crates at him, stalked into the now-empty garage, and hit the button, closing the door.

Now he was carless *and* homeless.

Nikki had said he was one of those people who couldn't hold on to anything nice.

She'd been wrong.

He couldn't hold on to anything at all.

After Angie kicked him out, Cam was full of pent-up rage. It wasn't that he blamed her—she was just being smart. He was pissed at *himself* for dragging her into this mess. With his mom gone, she was one of the few people in the world who actually gave a crap about him, and he sure as hell didn't want anything bad to happen to her or Joey.

But he still felt angry—at the universe for his mom getting sick, at his father for the fact that they'd been up to their ears in debt before she'd even been diagnosed. At the Tong for obvious reasons.

Parkour seemed the perfect distraction.

First, he stashed everything he owned in the corner of the break room at Lafayette. Then, he headed for the closest park and started practicing his cat leaps using the low wall at the perimeter. When that move felt solid, he started to use the benches to work on his dash vault.

As darkness started to fall, Cam realized he was getting tired, and he decided to head home.

And that's when he remembered he didn't actually have one anymore.

He snuck back into the break room at Lafayette Messenger and spent the night on the lumpy old couch, still leaping and jumping all through the night, in his dreams.

SIX

CAM SAT ALONE, looking down at the alley, watching a stray cat picking through a pile of garbage.

He'd woken up early, before anyone came into work at Lafayette. He was stiff from the training and from sleeping on the lumpy couch. He spent the morning finding a new place to crash—finally settling on an old seven-story building that was in foreclosure. Just the other day, on a delivery run for Lafayette, he'd spotted the place. It must have been a really nice place, once. There was even a small greenhouse on the roof. One of the glass walls had been broken, probably in a storm, but someone had draped a tarp over the opening to cover it. He had found a few old mattresses in the building, but with the nights so hot lately, Cam was betting it would be a bit cooler on the roof, so he dragged the least objectionable-looking mattress up and laid it under the tarp.

Now, as darkness was falling on another crappy day, he was enjoying his penthouse view.

The accommodations were pretty rough, but he figured this place would do until he could figure something else out—or until he got caught squatting there. He might have a couple of months or just one more day. Spotting the place to begin with had been dumb luck, random chance.

He was beginning to think that was all there was to life: dumb luck and random chance. Up to now, nothing anyone had ever tried to teach him had done him any good.

His life up to this point had been an extreme waste. That much was clear.

He lay back, crossed his arms, and looked up at the sky. Up this high, he could see a handful of stars. He spotted the Big Dipper—or maybe it was the little one? And that bright star might be Sirius, the Dog Star. Cam remembered when he was in grade school his class would go on field trips to the planetarium down the street. They'd lean back in their seats and gaze up at the fake stars glinting in the fake-sky ceiling. The guy who ran the place would teach them about the constellations, and tell stories about them. He remembered the man promising them that they could all be astronauts when they grew up, if they worked hard enough.

Cam closed his eyes, shutting out the stars. He'd worked hard ever since his mom had gotten sick, and look where it had gotten him. All the other useless things they'd tried to teach him in school—algebra and world history and Shakespeare— what had any of it been for? His tenth-grade girlfriend, Melina, had been obsessed with *Romeo and Juliet*—she'd made him watch the movie with Leonardo DiCaprio over and over before she even let him get to second base. She used to walk around quoting the lines all the time—telling him he was her Romeo. Cam knew what had become of Melina. He sure as hell hadn't turned out to be her Romeo, and neither had anyone else. All her faith in true love hadn't gotten her anything but pain and trouble. The boyfriend after him had gotten her into drugs; last he'd heard, she was serving a ten-year stint upstate for felony possession.

His parents had been the same, Cam mused—believing in fate and love and all the rest. He remembered his father taking him for a drive one night. They'd lain across the hood of the GTO, looked up at these same stars, and his father had explained to Cam how he would know when he'd met the right girl.

"It's magic, Cam," his father told him. He handed Cam the bag of Cheetos they'd been sharing, and wiped the orange dust from his hands. "That's what happened with your mother. She was manning the counter at her dad's place—remember the shop he had over in Elmhurst? Anyway, I took one look and *boom*. A goner. Got hit with Cupid's arrow, right between the eyes. I knew right away we'd be together forever. Magic, I'm telling you. It'll be just the same for you someday."

Forever got a lot shorter a few months later when his dad got sent to prison. Cupid's arrow had blinded his mom to his dad's faults until it was too late; all their money was gone and they were alone with his debts. And then she got sick.

So Cam was glad he'd learned so much valuable crap about love and sonnets and the freaking stars. It was all proving super useful.

The worst part: it seemed pretty clear now that Cupid had had the nerve to shoot *him*, two weeks ago. Except instead of an arrow, he'd gotten hit with an actual girl falling out of the sky.

Now Cam knew what he hadn't understood on that night long ago with his dad. Even if there *was* such a thing as love at first sight, the world was still going to tear the two of them apart, because that's what the world did. And he knew from watching that stupid movie with Mel where Romeo's love had gotten him.

Cam picked up a little glass pot that was sitting near the edge of the roof. It was pretty: red and gold glass panes in diamond shapes. The plant inside had died, but the roots were still there, tangled up in the dirt. He looked down. The cat was gone, the alley empty. Cam held the pretty thing up and then let go, watching the pot burst apart in the light of the street lamps below. He realized then that the glass had been broken and had cut into his hand. Now he would need to find something to bandage it. But at the moment he couldn't make himself move, or care. He lay back against the cold cement of the roof and stared out into the darkness.

The text message from Jax pulled Cam out of his thoughts:

Jets game & grub @ my place-104B Ave C @ 7

Cam smiled down at his phone. It had been forever since he'd gotten a come-hang-out text. He didn't hang out with any of the messengers at work.

His hand was still bleeding a little, so he ripped off the hem of an old T-shirt and wrapped it around his palm, then took the train down to Jax's place, which looked like one-quarter of a loft.

Jax answered the door wearing head-to-toe green and white. He clapped Cam on the back. "You made it! Welcome!"

"Thanks," Cam said. He walked in and looked around. There were three beds in one corner. "Nice place. You guys all live here?"

"Me and Tate and Dylan," Jax answered. "Oh, and my boys!"

At that moment, three pit bulls rushed toward Cam, almost knocking him over.

"I told you to hold them!" Jax called over his shoulder.

"I did," Tate yelled. "Noodle started slobbering all over me. Your dogs, dude. Control 'em."

Jax smiled sheepishly at Cam. "They told me if I bring home one more, I'm out," he confided. "They're rescues. I'm in this group, and they call me . . ." Jax shrugged as though to indicate his helplessness in the face of pit bulls in need. He led the way into the middle of the loft, where there were two big sofas and a flat screen already tuned in to the game.

"Told you before, dude. You gotta get your name off the sucker list," Tate said, standing and greeting Cam with a handshake. "Welcome to the dog pound. Have a seat. Hope you don't mind dog hair. Or drool."

"No worries," Cam said, sitting. One of the dogs promptly climbed up on top of him, staring at him with sad doggie eyes. He noticed that he only had three legs, and his ears looked like someone had attacked them with scissors. Cam reached up and petted his head. "Poor dude. Looks like you really needed a rescue," he said.

Jax sat down across from him. "Yeah, Sammy there had it the worst. He was a bait dog. People suck. But enough about my monsters. What do you like on your pizza?"

"Anything," Cam said. "I mean, I guess anything except pineapple. Pizza's just not the place for fruit."

"No arguments here," Tate said. "Dylan's on his way. With Nikki."

Cam wasn't sure how to feel about that news. Part of him wanted more time with her. Part of him just didn't understand her, and feared he never would.

Tate was calling for the pizza. "So you guys lived here long?" Cam asked Jax.

"Maybe a year? When I first came here I lived in this— *crap hole* doesn't begin to describe it. Finally, after meeting up with these guys, I went over to Tate's, and his place was a crack den too. So I had the idea we could go in together."

"Yeah, I've lived in my share of garbage places," Cam agreed. "You said you came here? From where?"

"Virginia, the bottom part—near Tennessee."

"*Why'd* you come here?" Cam asked. "No offense or any-thing. I've just spent most of my life trying to get out."

Jax seemed to consider the question for a few seconds before answering. "I started getting into tracing in my last year of high school. I was supposed to go to community col-lege, but really I just hated school. I was never any good at it. This was the first thing I was, like, good at—you know? Any-way, I knew this guy from my gym. He went to New York and got a job as a personal trainer, made huge money right out of the gate. Seemed like I should try my luck. I just wanted something . . . more, I guess."

"Well, you're doing pretty well for yourself," Cam told him. "What do you guys *do* for a living, anyway? Can't live off parkour."

Jax gave him a strange look. "You might be surprised." He got up and walked to the kitchen, coming back with a bone for each dog.

Cam watched him, thinking. It was obvious that the group did more than train together. But he knew he'd have to earn their trust before they told him their secrets. Especially if their business involved anything illegal.

Snapping back into the moment, Cam realized Jax was still talking to him. "Dude, you should have seen me the first couple months. Damn near starved to death." Another of the dogs jumped up beside Jax and he rubbed its head. "Good boy," he told the dog.

"You two wanna be alone?" Tate asked Jax.

"You're just jealous," Jax said. "When's the pizza coming?"

"Thirty minutes or less, just like always, moron."

They were interrupted as Dylan and Nikki came through the door. She was holding two paper grocery bags over her head, away from the dogs that crowded around her. Cam jumped up and took one of the bags from her and set it on the counter.

"What'd you bring us?" Jax asked her.

"Food."

"I mean, like, specifically?"

Nikki rolled her eyes as she put the remaining bag down on the table that separated the living area from the kitchen. "I *was* being specific. There's never any *food* in your food, so I brought you something with actual nutrition." She pulled out a plastic tray of veggies and waved it around like a flag. "See?"

Jax groaned. "I told you we should have ordered wings too."

Sighing, Nikki put the tray down on the kitchen counter. "Years from now, when your arteries are all clogged up, let it be remembered that I tried to save you."

Jax picked her up and twirled her around. "Ha! We're living fast here, baby. We don't worry about no stinking arteries."

"Put me down, you idiot!" Nikki demanded, and Jax complied. "Living fast? You know how that saying ends, right?"

"First she brings *vegetables*, then she brings the doom and gloom. Remind me again why you guys always want my sister around?" Dylan came up behind Jax and Nikki, used the counter to force the cap off his bottle of beer, pulled Nikki against him, and planted a kiss on the top of her head.

"Jerks," she muttered, but she was smiling.

"Game's on!" Dylan announced, as he headed for the TV.

"What did you do?"

Cam realized Nikki was talking to him. She pointed to the fabric he'd wrapped around his left hand.

"Training," he lied. He wasn't about to tell her he'd been wallowing in his own misery and cut his hand on a pretty glass flowerpot.

"You've been practicing," she repeated, her voice oddly toneless. Almost like she didn't approve.

"Yeah, some," he told her, keeping his own voice neutral. "It's kind of addictive."

Her face broke into a smile. "Yeah, it is. I never thought I'd like it—I did gymnastics when I was a kid, and at a certain point I started to hate it. The discipline, the hours and hours of practice. But parkour is different. No rules, you know?"

"You don't like rules, I take it?" he said, taking a step closer.

"Hey, you're bleeding!" Nikki took his injured left hand. Gently, she unwound the now-bloody strip of T-shirt. "You need to wash this out," she told him, and led him over to the kitchen sink.

"It's fine," Cam said, feeling embarrassed, as though by looking at the wound she'd be able to figure out he'd been lying about its source.

"Don't be such a tough guy, Cam. You don't want it to get infected."

"No. I don't want that." Cam was distracted. She had rinsed away the blood and was now gently drying his hand with a paper towel.

"I think they've got a first-aid kit down here." Nikki knelt down to open the cabinet under the sink. "Only because I *put* it here," she added, rolling her eyes and smiling as she stood up. She opened the small plastic case, found a big adhesive bandage, and pulled it out along with a packet of ointment. "This might sting a little," she said, carefully dabbing some of the antibacterial gel on his cut.

"It's fine," he said. Something had tightened in Cam's chest that made it hard to speak.

It was a little thing, her putting a bandage on his cut hand. But it had been a long time since anyone had taken care of him like that.

"There. All set. Just try to keep it dry until tomorrow."

"Thank you," he said, his voice coming out oddly hoarse.

"You're welcome." Nikki's eyes met his, and the moment stretched between them . . . but then that guarded look came over her face again.

She turned around and busied herself with pulling the plastic cover off the veggies, and the moment was over.

"You're missing the game!" Jax called.

"Coming," Cam said, but then turned back to Nikki. "Unless you need any help?"

"Nope. All set."

Cam sat down on one of the couches. He watched Nikki stop for a second, glance at the empty space beside him, and then choose a spot beside Jax on the other couch.

"You a Jets fan?" she asked Cam.

Yep, and we're having some great weather today too, Cam thought. He realized he was frowning when he saw his expression reflected on Nikki's face. "I guess not," she added.

"I'm really more of a Giants guy, actually," he said. The three-legged dog jumped up beside Cam again and he scratched its ears.

"Looks like you made a friend." Nikki smiled at him. The dog seemed to hear her, and chose that moment to sprawl out across Cam's lap, letting out a massive sigh.

"They say animals are good judges of character," she added.

Jax and Tate let out a loud cheer as the Jets made a field goal.

"Yeah, I guess so, although I'm starting to lose feeling in my leg," Cam replied, shifting his weight.

"Come here, Sammy," Nikki told the dog, patting her leg. All three of the dogs took that as an invitation, and they charged her. "No, I didn't mean—Noodle, get *off*!" She pushed at the biggest of the three, laughing.

"You're gonna have to burn those clothes," Tate said. "You know your roommate's not having that stink."

Nikki froze; she looked uncomfortable. She didn't quite meet Cam's eyes when she offered her one-word explanation: "Allergies."

The arrival of the pizza broke the strange mood Tate's comment had created, and Cam was distracted by the food and conversation. He realized how long it had been since he'd done anything as simple—and nice—as sitting around with a bunch of friends, eating pizza and watching a game.

When the game was over, and every scrap of pizza was gone (and even a few of the vegetables), Dylan invited Cam to train with them the next day.

On the train home, Cam was still smiling—at Jax's stupid jokes, at Dylan's perfect impression of that insurance lizard from the commercials—but mostly he was just smiling because he felt, for the first time in forever, like he wasn't completely alone.

There was even someone who cared enough to tell him not to get his bandage wet before his cut healed. If only he could figure out what was going on between them—and why she was always shutting him out.

SEVEN

CAM WOKE up choking.

The dream had started out the same as always. He'd been having nearly the same one, over and over, since that desperate day, one of the last of his mother's life, when he'd finally gotten up the nerve to borrow money from the Tong. He couldn't count the times he'd replayed the scene, the day he accepted the money, and the terms attached to it. He'd met his contact, Kai—Jerry's predecessor—in an abandoned theater on Division Street. Standing in front of an empty stage, listening to Kai's warnings, dream-Cam kept nodding, just as he had in real life. Just like on the real day, there had been no documents to sign. Hu had been there: standing like a sentinel, arms crossed, face frozen in his permafrown. In a way,

Hu *was* the terms of the loan. Pay the money back: good. Don't pay it back: Hu.

Cam had never asked what happened to Kai, but the guy still had a recurring role in his nightmares. This time, his face kept shifting back and forth. One minute he was Kai; the next minute he seemed to shrink and grow younger, and he was Jerry. Jerry/Kai was telling him how they'd find him if he didn't pay.

"It doesn't matter where you go," Jerry/Kai told him, smiling as his face changed yet again. "You understand?"

Cam was nodding. "I understand."

In the dream, he understood that this was a mistake. He knew the outcome . . . that it wasn't going to be enough to save the house anyway, that it was going to wreck his life, but when he tried to say he'd changed his mind, he just started coughing. It was like his throat was full of sand.

All this was a normal part of the dream, familiar even. But then something changed.

Suddenly, Cam heard the sound of laughing. He turned to see that it was Hu.

Hu never laughed.

The reason for the laughter soon became clear. His eyes followed Hu's up to the stage. A moment ago it had been hidden in darkness, but now the lights were on. In the bright spotlights, his new friends were posed like performers frozen in a tableau. There was Jax, sitting on the floor, his arms wrapped around his dog Noodle. There was Tate, holding a slice of pizza. And center stage, Dylan stood behind Nikki, frozen in the act of planting a kiss on the top of her head, as he had the day before.

But they were dead. They didn't move or speak or breathe; the cold pallor of their faces and their blue lips made it clear what Cam was seeing. Dream-Hu's laughter grew louder. Cam tried to speak but he found that his throat really was full of sand. He couldn't scream—he couldn't even breathe.

Jerry/Kai moved so that his face was close to Cam's.

He repeated the promise Jerry had made to him just two days before:

"If you don't pay, *we don't shoot* you, *Cam.*"

The horror of the dream stayed with him for the rest of the night. Without question, the idea of anyone getting hurt because of his mistakes with the Tong was a horrible one. But it was the image of Nikki's dead eyes in her frozen, blue-white face that would not leave him.

Maybe he cared even more than he'd realized.

His heart continued to race the whole ride down to the cargo ship. Cam thought maybe he'd just have a heart attack and that would be the end of it.

The dream hadn't just rattled him. No, he was plain old afraid.

Maybe dreams could be warnings. If so, then the message was clear: he had to pay back his debt. He thought briefly about just cutting ties with his new friends, but what if Jerry and Hu had already followed him? He'd been hanging out with them for days now.

He'd planned to keep hanging out with them—earn their trust. Find out about their business—the one Miller seemed to be grooming him for. Weigh his options and decide if what Miller had going was worth the risk.

But now he was out of options, and time. The only solution was money—no matter what he had to do to get it.

Cam burst into the "clubhouse" on the cargo ship unannounced.

Dylan, Tate, Jax, and Nikki were playing Ping-Pong. Nikki saw him first. She missed the ball.

"You okay?" she asked.

Cam tried to ignore her, looking right at Dylan. "I want in."

"You *are* in. We don't let just anybody train with us."

"No. I'm talking about work. Whatever you guys got going on, I want in on it."

"You okay, dude? You seem kind of . . . strung out." Dylan was looking closely at him.

Cam forced himself to inhale, exhale. Stop acting like a crackhead. "I'm fine. I just want in."

Dylan was still staring at him intently. Nikki looked up at her brother, her eyes huge.

"What's your problem?" Cam demanded, keeping his eyes on Dylan. "Do you guys think I'm a narc or something? Come on."

Nikki grabbed Dylan's arm; she was staring at him. "It's a bad idea," she told her brother, her tone insistent.

"Why?" Dylan looked down at her. "You know something I don't?"

She glanced nervously in Cam's direction, then back at her brother. Throwing her hands up in defeat, she stomped off.

Cam stared at her retreating figure, watching Dylan pull out his phone and make a call he knew was to Miller. Cam felt detached from what was happening. He wasn't nervous or excited.

He was just out of options.

◆ ◆ ◆

A little over an hour later, Cam was forcing himself to stay focused. Miller was explaining to him what being *in* meant. In detail.

Miller, it turned out, was one of those guys who was pretty freaking fond of the sound of his own voice.

"We're in the transport business, Cam. We move valuables. The difference is, I provide assurances that other people can't. I *guarantee* the work. You want some evidence to disappear? We can take care of that for you. It's a profession. We're not thrill seekers who pull any score that comes along. The key is speed . . . and silence. In and out, fast and quiet. We do our research, plan every move. Work as a team. Everyone knows their job. Documents, chemicals, technology. Anything. We don't take sides."

Cam nodded, making sure he looked like he was paying attention. But really, it was like he'd told Miller the day before. He really *didn't* care what was in the package. The only side he was on was his own. Dylan and Nikki had brought him to see Miller, but they were hanging back, just out of earshot. Nikki was pacing around the warehouse. (So far all of Miller's business seemed to be conducted in abandoned buildings.)

Miller had stopped for breath (everyone had to some-time), but then he continued: "I've just got two rules. One: you get in trouble, I'm your first call. Second: stay away from Chinatown. You stay out even if you're not on the job."

"How come?" Cam asked. He couldn't help it—that was the first interesting thing the guy had said.

Clearly, though, it had been the wrong question. Miller gave him a death glare. "This is my family, Cam. I'm inviting you to pull up a chair and sit down at our table. Show me you know how to be a good guest."

Cam nodded dutifully. Miller nodded too, and stalked off.

Great, Miller had dumped a whole load of Philosophy of Stealing on him, and he still didn't have the details on an *actual* job.

Dylan met his eyes. "Don't worry. That's just Miller. You're in. I'll text you the details of our next job soon." He looked from his sister to Cam, and then walked out of the warehouse.

Nikki was still pacing. "So that's it," Cam said into the silence that stretched between them. "Easy so far."

She stopped pacing and whirled to face him. "Easy? You're in the wrong place if you think what we do is *easy.*"

Cam closed the distance between them in a few short strides. He could tell he'd surprised her. She looked up at him, her eyes huge. "Well, you make it look easy," he told her, his voice low.

Nikki opened her mouth as if to speak, but she sort of sputtered instead, clearly still angry—or frustrated. "I . . . well, it's not. You shouldn't be here. You don't have to . . ."

"You don't know anything about what I have to do," Cam told her.

Nikki flinched. "No . . . I just mean, I want to warn you . . ."

He took another step. They were almost touching. "So warn me."

She stared at him. Her silvery blue eyes shone in the dim light coming through the dirty windows of the warehouse.

Cam moved slowly, putting one hand on her waist. She didn't move away; instead she closed her eyes, exhaling a ragged breath. "Cam . . ."

"Tell me to stay away," he breathed.

Her eyes flew open. She stared at him for a few more seconds, breathing in and out like she'd been running for miles. "I can't," Nikki choked out. She broke away from his light hold, and ran out the way her brother and Miller had gone. Cam stood still, frozen. Excited that she'd said "I can't," but confused about why she'd run away—again.

By the time Cam walked out of the warehouse, they were gone.

EIGHT

THE NEXT MORNING he got a text from a 917 number he didn't recognize.

It was short: u want to train later?

There were only two people in the group he hadn't exchanged numbers with: Miller and Nikki. If the message was from the former, Cam was definitely not in the mood to play eager student to Miller's Mr. Miyagi.

If the invitation was from the latter, well, he wasn't sure what his attitude actually *was* regarding mystery girl. Sometimes it seemed pretty clear that she was interested in him. The bike, for one thing. But it was also obvious that she didn't want him involved in the group's real business. Was she worried about him because she cared—or was there something else going on?

His phone buzzed again, and he read the message: This is Nikki btw.

Cam sighed, relieved that at least he knew who was on the other end of the invite now.

But now that he knew it *was* Nikki, his mind flew back to their last awkward moments the day before. She'd said she wanted to warn him not to get involved with Miller's business—she wanted to tell him to walk away.

"*I can't*," she'd finally said.

Cam stared at the phone in his hand like it was some kind of live explosive. Finally, he wrote back: Sure. Where?

You Pick.

ok. Riverside Park at 103rd-1 hour?

☺ c u there.

Cam shook his head and pocketed his phone. He decided to head uptown early. He could get in some practice before she got there.

He was heading for the door when he remembered to do a T-shirt check.

Even though he was headed out to run, he didn't want to smell horrible when he first got there. He grabbed a clean shirt and threw it in his duffel, then headed out to make a pit stop at the Y a few blocks away (his squat was conveniently priced at *free*, but whoever owned the place hadn't been thoughtful enough to keep paying the water bill).

Thanks to his decision to shower *before* getting sweaty, Nikki was already waiting for him in the park when he walked up. She was stretching, using one of the wrought-iron benches to help her balance.

She didn't see him yet, so he watched her for a few moments. Her movements were graceful, but she still seemed aware of her surroundings—watchful, maybe even wary. An older man was walking slowly through the park, close to the river, and he watched her eyes follow the man's progress.

She lifted her arms above her head in a slow stretch, turned, and spotted Cam. He didn't know why she'd texted him—what she wanted from him, if anything. He didn't understand why she was so closed off. But if the sudden smile on her face wasn't real, Cam didn't know what in this world was.

"You're late," she told him, but her smile stayed in place.

"Had to make a pit stop," he said, closing the distance between them.

As soon as they stood close together, he felt the tension from their last encounter flare between them. Her smile turned tentative. When he spoke again, his voice didn't sound as sure as he meant it to. "I was surprised you texted."

Nikki's eyes widened. "Oh. Well, I just thought . . . you said you'd been practicing. I guess I figured we might as well go together."

As explanations went, it was pretty noncommittal, but whenever Cam pushed her, even the slightest bit, she seemed to retreat back into her protective shell, like a spooked turtle. So he took one step away from her, stretching his arms, and steered the conversation back to a neutral topic. "So I think I'm pretty good on tic-tacs, kong vaults, and dash vaults. Any idea what I should tackle next?"

"Have you tried a palm spin?"

Cam shook his head. "I haven't seen that one."

"Well, you've seen Tate do it, for sure—he's, like, obsessed with them. But he mixes them in with lots of other moves, so you might not have noticed. It takes a lot of core strength, so not everyone can do it. Jax can't. But you said you used to do martial arts, right?"

He nodded. "Yeah. I can probably do it. Show me."

"Okay, first we need a low wall. Any of those around?"

"Couple blocks up, there's a wall around a bunch of playground equipment."

It was Nikki's turn to nod. "Okay, let's head up there. Just shout when we get to the spot." She took off at a run, safety-vaulting over a line of benches. Cam shook his head, smiling. It wasn't exactly easy to keep up with Nikki. Which was maybe the thing he liked best about her. He followed her lead, clearing each bench and picking up speed until they hit one where a woman was sitting, reading a book.

"Down here!" Cam yelled, spotting the little playground close to the water.

Nikki slowed her momentum and ran up beside him.

She put her left hand on the low wall in front of her. "So you're left-handed, which means you want to start with your right hand."

So she'd noticed he was a lefty. He forced himself to tune back in to her tutorial.

"Hey, is your cut healed enough to try this? I almost forgot."

Cam's breath caught for a second. He met her eyes and said, "Yeah. It's healing fine."

Nikki stared back for a few seconds before continuing. "Okay. So you put your weaker hand on the wall, fingers away from you. Then put your other hand on the edge, like this. Your thumb and palm go on the wall, your fingertips pointing back to you. See?"

Cam nodded, but she was already grabbing his right hand and dragging it over to the wall. She moved his left hand and positioned it the way she'd described. "Good. Now you jump—both feet. Use your right hand to push off the wall. Push yourself around, and land back on the same side where you started. When you do it for real, you'll approach the wall at a pretty fast run."

"I think I *have* seen Tate do this, actually."

"You wanna try?"

He just smiled.

She gave him a considering look. "Yeah, I didn't expect you to wimp out. Okay, back up, get some speed—now go!"

He took off, followed her directions, and executed the move—he suspected he'd done it perfectly. Cam stepped back. Based on Nikki's expression, he knew he was right. "Nice," she said, finally. "It took me like ten tries to even get the whole rotation."

Cam grinned. "What can I say? I'm a fast learner. Or maybe you're just a good teacher."

She smiled shyly. "No. I just have to learn all the moves this way—break them up into each little part . . . and someone has to explain them to me. You could probably have watched Tate do it full speed and then just copied him. I've seen you do that already with some other moves."

"Oh, have you?" he asked, stepping closer to her. "So you've been paying attention to my moves?" he added in a lower tone.

She laughed, but it sounded a little fake. She reached up and put a hand on his chest, lightly pushing him away from her. "Try it again. Maybe it was beginner's luck."

"Doubt it," Cam said, and backed up to go again. He did it once more. Perfectly, just like the first time. Then he moved back, ran up to the wall to go again. He slapped his hand down, started to jump, then let out a howl of pain and dropped to the ground. He lay there on his back, moaning.

"Oh my gosh, Cam! Are you okay? Did you pull something?"

She knelt beside him, her concerned face only inches from his, and he smiled up at her. "Gotcha."

"You jerk!" She pushed at his chest again, but this time he caught her arms. He started to pull her closer to him—very slowly, because it was so easy to spook her.

And then the rain started. It was a freakishly sudden shower. One moment, it was cloudy but clear—the next, there was a downpour. He stood up and grabbed her hand. The sudden, drenching rain made it seem less like a momentous choice than a way to stay together. It was hard to see, the rain was falling in such solid sheets. They ran, and began to laugh at the futility of it. There was no shelter anywhere close to them, and they were already soaked to the skin.

He pulled her along with him, back toward the playground.

The mulch soup on the playground was hard to walk in. Cam's sneakers sunk down into a hole, and his entire foot got wet. There was a space underneath the playground equipment where they could escape the rain. They had to duck down and crawl inside, one at a time. Cam let Nikki go first, then he crawled in after her. They barely fit in the tight space, but at least they were out of the pelting rain. She shivered, and he shifted closer to her. Nikki's arms were around her knees. "I can't believe this rain," she breathed. "This is like a Florida storm."

"Yeah, there's usually a bit of a drizzle first," he agreed.

She nodded. "This just came crashing in. There was no warning."

"That's kind of how I feel about you," he told her.

Her head shot up, and she bumped it on the hard plastic of the jungle gym.

"Are you okay?" he asked, laughing.

She raised a hand toward her head, but he was faster.

Gently, he ran his hand over the back of her head. "I don't think you'll have a bump."

"Ouch," she said, wincing. She closed her eyes. "You must think I'm a complete moron."

His hand was still resting on the back of her head. He slowly pulled a strand of wet hair away from her face and tucked it behind her ear. "I don't think that," he said.

She looked up at him, her eyes huge again, like she was amazed, or afraid. Or both. "I don't know anything when it comes to you," she told him.

Cam snorted. "That's my line."

"I'm sorry." The words seemed to burst out of her. There were raindrops falling from her hair down over her face. But she sounded so upset when the words spilled out of her, there might also have been tears.

He took a deep breath, trying to figure out what to say. But she kept going: "I know I'm always messing things up for you."

"I don't . . . you're not." He took a deep breath before pressing further. "I do have one question, though."

"Just one?"

Cam raised an eyebrow. "Okay, I have about a hundred. But one I want to ask you now. Why did you text me? Why are you helping me train?"

Nikki was staring at him, like she didn't know how to answer. Or didn't want to answer. "I was just being friendly."

"Liar," Cam said softly. "Why won't you tell me the real reason?"

She hugged her knees tighter. "I just wanted to, okay? There's no huge secret or anything."

"There's something you're not telling me."

She frowned. "I guess it was that cut you had on your hand the other day. You remember? How I helped you clean it and stuff?"

"Yeah . . ." Cam wasn't following, but he waited to hear what she had to say.

"When I helped you . . . I mean, I didn't even do that much. But I just keep thinking back to that look on your face."

"What look?" Cam asked, his voice coming out rough and uneven.

She raised her eyes to meet his. "You looked so . . . grateful? Like nobody's taken care of you in a really long time."

He swallowed past the sudden lump in his throat. "Yeah. I guess it has been a while."

When she didn't respond after a few seconds, he added, "So that's why you texted me. Because I seemed so pathetic."

"No! God, Cam, that's not what I meant. I shouldn't have told you . . . I just meant, it seemed like maybe you . . . just forget it." She was moving now, trying to squeeze past him, out of the small space.

He reached out to put a hand on her arm. "Nikki . . ."

She looked up at him, her eyes pleading. "Let me go."

It felt like the words meant more than just *move over.* He took his hand away from where it rested on her arm. If she wanted to go, he would let her.

Apparently she wanted to.

She crawled out first. The rain had slowed. He struggled out behind her, and she reached a hand out to help him up— not meeting his eyes. "I'm sorry you got soaked. I'll be sure to check the weather next time," she said.

"You can't predict everything," he told her.

He knew what was coming, so he turned and walked away first.

As he rode the subway downtown, Cam tried to forget the strange workout session with Nikki, pushing the weird encounter into a little box in the back of his mind. He had to focus on getting paid, and getting out from under his debt.

Cam made his way over to Lafayette Messenger to ask

Lonnie for a leave of absence. Miller had made it clear he needed Cam to be ready for a job at a moment's notice. He'd also made it pretty clear that no one in the group had a second job—and neither should Cam.

"Leave of absence?" Lonnie repeated. "What is this, Trump Tower? You work or you quit. Which is it?"

Cam glared at him. "Well, given my limited options, I'm gonna have to go with *quit.* I told you, I found a second job. You know I need the money."

"And I'm telling you, go ahead and consider it your *only* job," Lonnie snapped, before calling out for a messenger to deliver a hot run to 48th and Lex.

"Thanks a lot, Lon," Cam said, walking away. A young guy Cam didn't know was biking up to the counter to pick up the run Lonnie had announced, but, as he reached out for the package, he lost control of his bike and wiped out right in front of Lonnie and Cam. "I can see why you'd be so anxious to get rid of me," Cam added.

Lonnie didn't say anything, and Cam walked back out to the street. He kept going for a few blocks, wondering how much money he should let himself spend on lunch. The growling in his stomach was definitely calling out for more than two hot dogs, which was his usual budget. He headed toward Walker Street, where there was a pretty decent/cheap noodle house. An Asian man jumped in front of him as he walked—only his recently-sharpened-by-parkour reflexes kept him from running into the guy.

"Take a look, many nice things," he said, motioning to a pair of tables. The man was incredibly short—he came only to Cam's chin, and Cam wasn't exactly tall.

He took a step back away from the little guy. "Some sales technique," he told him. He was feeling surly after Lonnie's dismissal. "Knocking people over isn't gonna make them want to buy your crap."

"No crap!" The man looked highly offended. "Quality merchandise. I have store—down Cortlandt Alley. You have seen, maybe? Nice place. Landlord is a bastard—raise the rent too high. Now all my nice items for sale here, under the sky." The strange little man gestured upward, then performed a sort of bow.

Cam chuckled. In spite of himself, he felt bad for the guy. Some fat cat probably *had* raised his rent higher than he could pay. After all, the same thing had happened to his mom at least twice.

He shrugged and walked over to the guy's tables. "So what have you got?" Cam asked, more out of pity than anything else.

"Many nice things!" The man's face broke into such a wide smile that Cam realized he was going to *have* to buy something.

That was the problem with showing a shred of human decency, sometimes. It was hard to stop at just one shred.

The first table was filled with ceramic pots, mugs, candle holders, and other tchotchkes. Cam kept walking and looked at the second table, which was covered in jewelry. For some reason, one of the necklaces caught his eye. It was a silver pendant: a tiny little bird in a fancy cage, suspended on a long, thin silver chain. It reminded him right away of Nikki. That trapped look she'd had under the jungle gym, maybe. Or maybe it was the way she never seemed to feel free to say what she really wanted to say.

"How much for this?" he asked the man.

"I make you good deal. Thirty-five."

"I can do twenty," Cam told him, knowing the guy had aimed high. It was probably worth closer to ten, but now he was feeling charitable.

The man pretended to think it over, then nodded and began wrapping up the necklace. He dropped it into a tiny canvas bag decorated with little green leaves. Cam handed him the cash.

"Thank you so very much," the man said, bowing again.

Cam thought he saw tears in his eyes. Cam nodded and hustled away before he gave the guy any more of the money that technically belonged to Chen.

That was the thing about this city. You could be walking along, just hoping for some lunch, minding your own business, and something right there on the sidewalk could break your heart.

NINE

FOR THE REST of the day, Cam kept the bird pendant stuffed in his pocket, and the confusion Nikki made him feel locked up in that box in his mind. He needed to get some sleep in case Miller called with a job, as he'd hinted he might. Cam told himself that if he could get clear of his debt, maybe then he could go back to trying to figure out the Nikki puzzle.

The call he'd been waiting for came at five o'clock that afternoon, and just like that, Cam was in. *Breaking* in—getting his feet wet with a little felony B and E. They'd picked him up just after three in the morning and driven him out to a remote part of Long Island. Now he and Dylan were rushing through the dark, past rows of metal cages. They were moving fast (extreme speed being the best skill on Cam's résumé), but not so fast that he didn't see the sign that hung above the cages: SUFFOLK COUNTY FEDERAL EVIDENCE LOCKER.

It was a safe bet the cops would have zero sense of humor about anything taken from this place. So Cam tried to block everything out of his mind except for following Dylan's lead: fast and silent. They accessed the building through a maintenance shaft in the roof.

He wondered briefly how Miller had even known this place was *here*. From the outside, the building looked like an old, abandoned manufacturing plant: peeling gray paint and dirty, broken windows, some boarded up, some just crisscrossed with duct tape. The inside was a vast warehouse crammed with row after row of huge metal shelves. Dylan dropped down from the rafters next to a shelf marked with the number 921, and Cam followed, landing in a crouch, as much like a silent cat as he could manage. He envied people like Miller and Nikki, who were thinner than he was, more graceful. Cam was more compact and muscular. Probably no one would ever call him catlike.

Cam forced himself to focus. Although the actual words his brain used were *stop thinking about Nikki, you moron*.

Dylan tapped his shoulder, pointing to a security camera. Cam felt a stab of cold fear in his stomach, but then he realized the camera was pointed down at the floor. He didn't stop to wonder why anyone would record the floor; he just kept following Dylan down the row of shelves. Each item was tagged with its own yellow sticker.

Cam scanned the numbers on the first shelf, moving fast, then spotted the number they were looking for: 6453. A small box sealed with yellow tape. Cam thrust the box inside his backpack, then shrugged his shoulders back into the straps. Just then a small beam of light passed over their heads: a guard's flashlight. They melted into the darkness inside the cage, behind the first row of shelves, barely breathing. Cam felt another stab of cold fear. He closed his eyes and for a few moments it was like he'd traveled outside his body. He was in the past; his bare feet cold on the concrete floor of his cell back in Otisville. He heard one of the guard's belligerent voices bark his name.

Cam's mind snapped back to the present. He could not go back there. He had to stay focused. The flashlight's beam became more distinct as it came closer, the sound of footsteps accompanying the light. They heard the crackle of the guard's radio, then the man grunted, "All clear." In a few moments, the light was gone, and the footsteps faded into the distance.

They surged forward, headed back the way they had come, but another crackle of the radio and a brighter beam of light sent them flat onto the concrete floor.

"Base to walker, you check the East Hall?"

Cam felt his pulse jump at the sound of the voice over the radio, echoing loud in the quiet warehouse.

"Roger. All clear."

"I got movement down there," the voice on the radio shot back. "I'm headed your way."

Dylan motioned to Cam, and they both began the silent crawl away from the guards' voices. They kept moving, shimmied up a support beam, then swung back up into the rafters. Cam allowed himself one quick look down. The clueless guards were shining their flashlights everywhere *except* above their heads.

Cam followed Dylan out of the hatch in the roof they'd used to enter the building, gasping as he let himself really exhale for the first time in what felt like hours. Dylan turned to smile at him. "Good job."

Cam nodded, smiling back, not letting himself think of anything beyond Dylan's words. They *were* out. He had done a good job. They were walking across the roof, Cam's breath returning to normal, but then he saw Dylan tense ahead of him. That's when the three men in masks came out of the darkness. They were on the other side of the roof, moving fast. Cam saw that at least one of them was holding a gun. His throat closed, and his heart sped up again. But again he closed his eyes and forced himself to stay in control. A strange feeling of detached calm came over him.

He'd always been able to do this—step a little outside himself, and just solve the problem.

He and Dylan both started running—by unspoken agreement, heading in two different directions. Cam scrambled for the edge, vaulting over to the next building like his life depended on it. Which maybe it did.

Two guys pursued Dylan—leaving one following Cam. But one was more than enough. The guy was fast. And he had a gun. Cam cleared his mind of everything except the path ahead. He crossed the neighboring building in seconds, vaulting onto the next one; then he spotted the fire escape and used his traction to hurtle himself down onto a balcony. He tried the double doors; he was shocked when one opened, but didn't stop to bask in the good luck—just kept sprinting, full out, through an abandoned food court, between the tables and chairs, coming up short before a sudden drop to the next level. He almost tripped on a folding plastic warning sign: WET FLOOR. *Thanks a lot,* he thought. But then he was hit with a sudden inspiration—he threw the plastic sign under his feet like a skateboard and rode it down the escalator.

The vibrations of the flat plastic on the ridged metal traveled through his bones; even his teeth rattled. But Cam still grinned on the way down. If he was about to be caught and sent to jail—or worse—at least he was going out with a stunt fit for a freaking cartoon superhero.

As the sign hit the floor, Cam jumped off, his legs hitting the ground hard, like a pair of stilts striking the concrete. He was barely able to stay on his feet. He heard the masked guy's heels pounding away behind him, so Cam picked up speed, sprinting across the empty store. He vaulted over a turnstile and flew out a pair of glass doors onto the street. It was starting to hurt to breathe—he felt spikes of pain attack his lungs—but he didn't slow down.

The sound of running was still behind him. He could not shake this guy.

He didn't know who the masked guy was—he couldn't be a cop. But whoever he was, once he caught Cam, he'd have the package. And Cam's short-lived career with Miller would be over.

His first foray back into the criminal world was already

going down the drain. He should have known better. His mother's face appeared in his mind's eye, and—not surprisingly—she was frowning. All she'd wanted for him was something *else.* She'd wanted him to *not* become his dad.

Inside his head, he whispered, *I'm sorry*, to his mother. Then he looked around the street for a possible escape route. There'd be plenty of time for apologizing to ghosts if he ended up becoming one himself.

But then: headlights. A van was headed his way. Cam leapt and managed to perch precariously on the back bumper of the van, holding on tight as it pulled away from whoever the man in the mask was.

The cold air washed over him like a baptism. He'd started a new life as a successful criminal—he hoped. He felt the relief start to flow through him.

Cam stayed on the van until he'd put a couple of miles between him and the scene of crime. He jumped down and crouched low, out of sight. Cam checked his pack to make sure the box had made it through the chase without falling out or getting crushed. He made his way to the pickup spot, which thanks to the ride he'd hitched was just a few blocks away. Then he checked his watch, trying to will time to move faster toward the rendezvous Miller had set. Now that he'd gotten away, he just wanted this first job to be over. He won-dered if Dylan had managed to shake his two pursuers.

Dawn was creeping in as Cam heard the tires crunch slowly toward his hiding place, nearly half an hour later. He checked his surroundings before crossing the street to meet the others. But it wasn't Miller's Escalade coming toward him—it was a white van. The back door was thrown open, and the masked figure he thought he'd shaken appeared behind him, and shoved him inside.

At first, Cam was too shocked to struggle—he'd been so sure he'd shaken the guy.

The van had come to a stop. Now he lay on his back on the floor, as Mask and three of his also-masked friends crowded around him, holding him down. Mask still had his gun, which was now pointed at Cam.

Cam struggled to get free, but it soon became clear that struggling was pointless.

Confusion was racing through him, but it was hard to think straight with a gun in his face.

"Hey," he protested, trying to move away from the gun.

"Shut up!" Mask barked.

"Don't," Cam heard himself say.

One of the others pulled the pack from his back, almost yanking his right arm from its socket in the process. Cam ground his teeth, not wanting to give them the satisfaction of yelping in pain. Mask ripped open the bag, pulling out the box. "Who do you work for?" he demanded, digging his weapon into the side of Cam's neck.

"No one."

"*Who?*" Mask demanded again, moving the gun upward so that it pressed into Cam's temple.

"Get off me!"

"What's in the box?"

"Nothing," Cam spit out. "I don't know what's in it."

The gun pressed harder into his temple. It was starting to seriously hurt. It was weird, but the man in the mask seemed almost to be smiling. He lowered his voice and asked again, this time in a menacing hiss, "Who do you work for?"

Cam stared back at him in stony silence.

He'd thought, for a few brief, shining moments, that he was safe. Later, he'd have time to wallow in self-pity. At the moment, he was just plain pissed off.

"You tell me what's in the box or I'm gonna blow your brains out. How about that?"

Cam glared mutinously. "I. Just. Carried. The. Box."

Bastard. He didn't say that last part out loud, since he didn't actually have a death wish.

For a few seconds, the dark eyes of the man in the mask stared into his. Cam closed his eyes. This was probably it for him. Sort of a fitting end, really. At least he'd gotten to pull that great trick with the WET FLOOR sign before he checked out.

I'm sorry, Mom. Those seemed like fitting last words, even if he could only say them inside his head.

Then he felt the metal of the gun lift away from his face. Someone patted him on the shoulder.

"Good work, Cam."

The man pulled off his mask: it was Miller.

The other masks came off to reveal Dylan, Tate, and Jax, all laughing.

Cam had lost sight of the gun, which was probably a good thing because his mood had just turned murderous.

"Hey, it's all right, buddy." Miller smiled at him. "We just had to make sure you had our backs. You're family now." He offered Cam a hand, since he was still lying on the floor of the van. "What do you think?"

Cam sat up on his own. "I think you're a bunch of jerks."

More laughs. Cam let out the breath he'd been holding,

stared at them for a few seconds, and then for some reason he started laughing too.

He was maybe just feeling relief, but it did feel good to laugh. And also: not being dead felt good too.

The jerks, all except Miller, took him out for pancakes. Initiation with a gun to your head, followed by a hearty breakfast. Cam suggested that they should make that the group's slogan—maybe get T-shirts made.

Jax agreed: "Yeah, good way to recruit."

Dylan threw a napkin at Jax's head. "Just how many folks you think Miller's looking to recruit?" he asked.

"Well, maybe we should get another girl. You know, for Niks," Jax answered.

"For me, huh? Thanks, Jaxy. You're a real gentleman."

Cam's head shot up and his eyes met Nikki's. He started to get up to make room for her, but he was too slow; her brother had already hopped out and grabbed himself a chair. Dylan pulled it up to the end of the booth and Nikki slid in across from Cam.

"So you passed," she observed, without really meeting Cam's eyes.

"Guess so," he said, looking down at the remains of his

breakfast. She'd left him in the rain. Or he'd left her first before she could. Whatever. He wasn't sure how happy he was to see her.

"Yeah, pay up," Dylan demanded.

Cam glared at Nikki. "You bet against me?" His voice came out a little too high-pitched. He *was* sure how he felt about the possibility that Nikki hadn't thought he'd pass his test. In a word: pissed.

Nikki's eyes widened. "No!" Cam watched the blush spread over her cheeks.

Tate put a wad of bills in Dylan's outstretched hand and gave Cam a shrug. "Nothing personal, brother. I thought you'd probably crack. The gun and all . . ."

"I probably would've taken that bet," Cam said, letting him off the hook. "I am sort of fond of my head," he added.

"Me too."

Cam's head swiveled toward Nikki. He didn't quite believe his ears. She'd said it so quietly, he couldn't even be sure he'd heard it. Dylan must not have—he was busy calling the waitress back over to take his sister's order.

"What do you want?" Dylan asked her.

She looked up and smiled, but her eyes were on Cam as she said, "Not sure yet."

◆ ◆ ◆

Cam pretended he was still eating and stayed behind when Dylan, Tate, and Jax rose to go. The waitress had just refilled Nikki's coffee, and she sat back down after letting Tate out of her side of the booth.

"You coming?" Dylan asked her.

Nikki stirred her coffee slowly. "I'll catch up with you later," she said, without looking up. Her voice sounded casual. Or like she was trying to make it *sound* casual. Dylan shot his sister a look, but he didn't say anything, just nodded.

"You did good," he told Cam. "Later."

"Thanks, man."

Why am I still sitting here? Cam wondered. As far as he could tell, he was sitting there trying to figure out the *motivation* behind Nikki's choice to stay. The rational part of his brain knew he should have gotten up from the booth and followed Dylan out of the diner.

He was an addict. That had to be it. He'd resisted alcohol, never fallen into the drug habit, but here he was, waiting to see what she would say next. Waiting for his next hit.

Nikki was still stirring her coffee instead of drinking it. She didn't look up as she observed, "So it's true. You never look inside the package?" She raised her eyes to meet his.

Morning sunlight was streaming in through the dirty windows of the diner. Cam noticed how long her lashes were as she blinked, then scooted a little farther into the booth, out of the blinding rays.

"Nope," he told her. "Never. Guess it's a good thing too, or I'd be dead now instead of having pancakes with a pretty girl."

He had the satisfaction of seeing her eyes widen in surprise at that one. "Come on," he told her. "You know you're pretty. Don't act surprised."

She opened her mouth, but didn't say anything right away, and closed it again. She started stirring again, though there couldn't possibly be any sugar crystals left undissolved in that mug. "I looked inside. Once." So she was skipping right over his calling her pretty.

He leaned forward across the table. "Oh yeah? Hopefully not on *your* initiation day? Or maybe you did, but Miller just thought you were too cute to shoot."

Nikki frowned at his words, but then quickly shook her head. "No—I never had an initiation," she said, the words coming out in a rush. Her voice sounded a little breathless.

"Too cute for that requirement?" he pressed.

"What is this obsession you have with my level of cuteness?"

Cam grinned at her. *Addict.*

"I wouldn't say obsession," he began. "Maybe more of an . . . interest."

Nikki was shaking her head. She took a sip of her now-cold coffee, and Cam thought her hands seemed unsteady as they held the mug—though he might have been imagining things. "Don't you want to know what I saw in the package?" she asked.

He didn't, actually, but he was starting to get used to Nikki's method of misdirection. He decided to play along. "Sure. What was in the package?"

"It was a solo job—Miller sent me alone to this guy's place."

Cam felt his jaw tighten.

Nikki noticed his reaction. "It's not what it sounds like—the guy was having a party. Anyway, it was this loft, in the Flatiron District. The guy had these paintings all over his walls. Really . . . they were just . . . beautiful. I've never seen anybody's actual home that looked like that. The thing I was supposed to grab, it was in this little cardboard tube, about this long." Nikki held her hands about two feet apart. "I figured that what was inside had to be another painting. And I'm leaving his place, and suddenly I just have this overwhelming urge to *see* it. So once I was clear of the place, I did—I opened the tube, unrolled what was inside."

"What was it?" Cam asked, when she didn't say anything more.

Nikki closed her eyes. "It was the ocean—just after a storm. All dark blues and yellows and purples. You know how the sky turns almost purple right after a storm? It looked like that." She opened her eyes. "I checked online, after I dropped it off with Miller. There was a missing Van Gogh that looked just like it . . ."

"No," Cam breathed. "Even *I* know who that is, and I'm not exactly an art guy. You're saying Miller actually *stole* a Van Gogh?"

She shrugged. "Well, first this art guy stole it. Or maybe I'm wrong. It's just a cool story now. One you can't *ever* tell Miller. Actually, don't tell anyone."

"You didn't tell your brother?"

"I've never told anybody."

"Thanks for picking me." he said.

Nikki nodded, her eyes on the table once more. "It's good you passed their test and all, but you're so set on just following orders, keeping your head down. You might be missing something—if you never look."

"I'm looking," he told her, and this time her gaze rose to meet his.

She understood, Cam could tell. Nikki didn't come up with one of her conversational detours right away, like she usually did—she just returned his stare. He felt a heat that had nothing to do with the morning sun filling their booth.

Nikki's voice was a little hoarse when she finally spoke: "On second thought, don't listen to me, Cam. You *should* keep your head down. You should stay safe."

She was out of the booth and gone from the diner before he could react. Cam stared at her empty coffee mug for a long time before heaving himself out of the booth and back onto the street.

TEN

THE VAN screeched to a halt a few feet from where Cam was sitting on the curb the next morning. He stood up and opened the door. Nikki was at the wheel, but she wasn't looking at him.

"Hey," he said.

He got a fairly frosty "hey" in return, but she still didn't turn his way, just put the van back in gear and started driving.

It definitely felt like the temperature had dropped overnight. Well, the *weather* was about the same as yesterday: it was Nikki who was suddenly a lot colder.

"Where are the others?" he asked.

"Busy."

One-word answers weren't very encouraging, but Cam kept pushing. "Well, you wanna grab a coffee or something?"

"This isn't a date."

"I didn't mean . . . I didn't mean it like a date."

And then he disgusted himself by stuttering.

"Let's just get this done," Nikki said, slamming her foot down on the accelerator, and steering the van toward the Queensboro Bridge.

"Where are we going?" Cam asked.

As they stopped at the first red light in Manhattan, she finally turned to face him. "Does it matter?"

Okay, he was definitely not imagining the ice. What the hell had happened since yesterday, when she'd told him about the painting?

"Do you mean, like, existentially?"

The light had turned green, but she glanced back over at him without accelerating. "'Existentially'? Thought you dropped out of high school."

He raised an eyebrow at her. "Yeah. But my brain still works." He leaned toward her across the seat and thumped his chest a few times. "Cam. Can. Read," he added in his best Tarzan voice.

The ghost of a smile almost cracked through her frozen exterior, but she mastered it fast. "We're here," she said, steering the van through the open door of a warehouse.

A compact, wiry man with a maze of scars crisscrossing

his face stepped out of the shadows and nodded toward them. Nikki jumped down, went around to the back of the van, and opened the doors. The man began to silently unload the boxes they'd brought. Nikki walked a few paces away and made no move to help the guy, so Cam shrugged and went to stand beside her.

He decided to test the icy waters. "So did you grow up in the city?" he asked.

"No."

Back to monosyllables. Not that she'd believe he knew what that word meant, Cam reflected. He decided to keep pushing. "So you and Dylan both decided to move here?"

"Yes."

"*Yes*, huh? Wow, that's very enlightening. So you moved to the city with your brother, but you guys don't live together. You've got that roommate, right? The one who's allergic to dogs . . ."

Nikki whirled to face him. "Enough questions, okay?"

"I'm just making conversation."

She cut him off. "You wanted to be in. Guess what? You're in." She sounded almost angry now. She started pacing away from him. "There's nothing left to discuss."

Cam didn't take time to think about his next words; they just burst out of him: "What's your deal?"

"My *deal*?" She spun on her heel and faced him. There was no mistaking the anger now. Her arms were crossed, her eyes narrow, her voice shook just a little.

Cam took a step closer to her; he was beginning to feel pretty angry himself. "Yeah."

"There's no deal."

"Then why are you acting like this?"

"Like what?"

"Like a freaking ice queen!"

"*Ice queen?*" Nikki repeated. Her voice was definitely shaking now. For a few seconds, she glared at him, her nostrils flaring, her chest heaving. Finally she took a deep breath, let it out, and resumed her pacing. Without warning, she strode up to him. They stood just a few feet apart. "I'm not the one who has a *deal*," she nearly snarled at him.

Cam decided to try a different tack. Lowering his voice, he said, "I don't know, I just thought we . . ."

Nikki cut him off. "I didn't ask you to come find me."

Cam took another step closer to her. He wanted to make her look at him. "You sure about that?" he asked, his voice still low. She met his eyes, but quickly looked away again.

He put a hand on her arm. "You gave me that bike," he pressed.

Her eyes met his again, and at that moment he saw a flash of pain. She looked as confused as she was making him feel. But then she stepped back away from him. Cam let his hand drop.

"I'll tell Miller you can work on your own next time," she said, her voice wooden. "You don't need a babysitter."

He stared after her as she stomped back toward the van. The guy had finished unloading, and she slammed the back doors with more force than was necessary. Nikki climbed back into the driver's seat. Cam heard the van start back up, and wondered briefly if she'd leave him behind if he didn't run to catch up.

It felt like he was always running to catch up to her.

He took his seat and reached for the door, but the un-loading guy closed it for him and tapped on the door. "This the new guy?" he asked Nikki.

"Yeah," she told him. At least Nikki offered equal-opportunity monosyllabic communication. But it didn't exactly make Cam feel any better.

The scarred man leaned his head through the open win-dow and grinned at him. "Good luck, new guy."

For some reason, the words sounded like a warning.

As they drove back over the bridge, a silence filled the

van, threatening to choke Cam. When they stopped near his place, he reached for the door and started to push it open, but then thought better of it. He pulled the door toward him again, closing it with a loud thud.

That got Nikki's attention. For just one second, he saw fear flare in her eyes. Was she scared of him?

That thought made him angrier than any of the rest of it. He kept his eyes down on his hands, which were balled into fists in his lap. He spoke slowly, trying to control his anger. "I don't know what happened to you . . . why you're . . . shut down. And you're right, I *did* come to find you. I can't change that. But I need this . . . my messenger job wasn't going to save . . . it wasn't cutting it, moneywise. So I guess you're stuck with me now. I'm sorry that's pissing you off." He looked over at her. She was staring at him with a miserable expression on her face, but she still didn't speak. "On second thought: forget that last part. I'm not sorry," he said, pushing open the door and jumping down to the street. "By the way, I got you this." He put the little canvas bag that held the bird-cage necklace on the passenger seat. He'd kept it with him. Some part of him had been waiting until the right moment to give it to her. But it was starting to become clear that the moment was never going to be right.

He didn't look back as the van pulled away from the curb and down the street.

Cam made it all the way upstairs before he realized his brain was missing.

Today was payday, the day he'd been waiting for, and he'd just let his ride down to the docks drive away.

Dramatic exit: 1. Free ride: 0.

Trying to figure out Nikki's sudden frost had distracted him. Unfortunately, he couldn't *afford* to be distracted. There was the small matter of his massive debt. His repoed car. And now he needed to refill his MetroCard just so he could go get paid.

He vaguely remembered something his father had told him a long time ago—a warning that girls can make you stupid.

On the ride across town, Cam glared at the floor of the train, making plans. He decided the first debt he needed to pay was the rent he owed Angie. She needed the money, he knew, and it wasn't her fault she'd rented her garage to a guy who was in debt to the Chinese Mafia.

When he arrived at the ship, Cam saw Jax sitting on the curb, legs crossed and head down. The guy was just staring at his shoelaces.

"What's up, man?" Cam asked, walking up to him.

Jax looked up. "Oh. Hey, Cam. Not much. Miller was looking for you. It's payday."

"So I heard. You don't sound excited."

He shrugged. "I'm excited."

Cam sat down beside him. "Then why do you sound like somebody swiped your puppy?"

Jax tried to smile. "Wouldn't mind another puppy." He shook his head. "No big thing. Just been . . . thinking."

"About?"

Jax scrubbed his hand through his bright red-orange hair, making it stand up in crazy spikes. "It's just, this guy I used to see sometimes working out . . . before I met Dylan and them. Today I see online that he's gonna be in a *movie*. An actual movie. He's tracing—like doing the stunts." When Cam didn't respond right away, Jax hurried on, talking fast. "It's not like I'm jealous or anything. But it sort of makes me wonder . . . if maybe I'd gone down a different route . . . I don't know . . ."

"I hear ya," Cam said, nodding. They sat in silence for a minute. "So you thinking of going straight?" he asked.

Jax's head twitched, and he laughed nervously. "No, man. Just having a moment. Don't . . . could you maybe not say anything about this? To Miller . . . or anybody?"

Cam met his eyes. "Course not. Besides, what's to tell? You're not the only one, Jax. I mean . . . I wish *I* could go straight. But I turned left when I should have turned right a long time ago."

Jax sighed. "Yeah. Know what you mean. See you later, Cam." He jumped up and started walking away, then turned back. "I'm glad you're in the group now. I mean, *I'm* glad . . . for, like, selfish reasons. Not that you're *in*, but . . . you know what I mean."

Cam smiled, but Jax was already walking away. The weird part was that Cam knew exactly what he'd meant.

Once Jax was gone, Cam made his way onto the ship. As he stepped into the clubhouse, Miller greeted him, then pulled out a stack of hundreds and counted out Cam's share.

"Membership has its privileges," Miller told him, handing him the stack. Cam forced himself to smile at Miller's comment. The guy didn't seem to like it when people failed to appreciate his cheesy sound bites.

"Thanks," Cam grunted. As he walked away, he looked down at the money in his hand, imagining what it would be like to hold on to it for longer than an hour. At least he could knock another two grand off what he owed to the Tong, after settling up with Angie for the rent. But when he took the interest into account, the possibility of getting out from under the debt still seemed very far away.

Angie's job made Cam's problems look fractionally less depressing: the place was literally a sweatshop; everyone inside was constantly wiping their streaming foreheads. Angie was seated in front of a sewing machine—the factory floor was crammed so full of tables and machines that he could barely make his way through the maze to get to her.

The moment she spotted him, Cam saw her stiffen.

"What are you doing here, Cam? I'm working."

"I brought you rent money."

He didn't miss her look of surprise.

Always nice to have people's low expectations of him confirmed.

Cam reached for his wallet. "I don't care what you brought," Angie spit out.

She got up and started walking fast, deeper into the interior of the factory. Cam followed her. Angie jerked open a door and stalked into what looked like some kind of break room. All the chairs were the plastic kind, like you find in high school classrooms. This place made Lafayette Messenger look like a country club.

Angie whirled around to face Cam as he pulled the cash out of his wallet. "Please take it," he pleaded. The thought of letting Angie down was more than he could take. Whenever he thought about the mess he'd gotten her and Joey into, he just kept picturing his mom looking at him in disappointment. She'd really liked Angie.

A massive sigh escaped Angie's lips as she accepted the stack and quickly counted the bills. "This is too much."

Cam let out his breath too, in relief. She was going to take the money. "It'll hold you until you find someone else to move in."

Angie looked up at him. "Oh, Cam. Your mom always told me what a good kid you were. I thought . . . forgive me, but I knew about . . . some of what you'd gotten into. I thought she was probably a little bit blind when it came to her baby. But she was right after all. You *are* a good kid."

Cam swallowed hard. Her words about his mom sliced through his heart. It hurt to breathe, all of a sudden.

"What kind of trouble are you in?" Angie asked, in a quiet voice.

Cam sighed. Jerry and the always-charming Hu had picked up Angie's kid and delivered him home as a warning to Cam. He owed her an explanation of why he was in trouble, at least.

He recited the bare bones of the story, fighting to keep the emotion out of his voice. He couldn't bear for her, or anybody, to pity him. What was done was done. "After Mom got sick, I borrowed some money off the street to try and help her keep the house. It wasn't enough. The bank foreclosed on it a week before she died."

Angie took a small step closer to him. Just as he'd feared, her eyes were filled with pity now, and it was almost worse than the distrust and anger from a few minutes ago. "You got a good heart, Cam. But you gotta be careful. The farther you go down the wrong road, the harder it is to find your way back."

Her words struck him like a slap. His mom had said almost the exact same thing to him in the last week of her life. No wonder they had gotten along so well.

And, to his shame, this past week had been all about finding a new road to lead him out from under his debt. An *illegal* road.

Another wrong path.

"I gotta get back to work," Angie told him.

Cam reached into his bag and pulled out a new skateboard. "Can you give this to Joey? You don't have to tell him it's from me."

He saw tears well up in Angie's eyes. "He misses you. I wish . . ."

"Me too," Cam said. "Hey . . . Ang . . . I'm sorry. About everything. I won't bother you guys again."

She touched his arm for just a second, smiled sadly, and then Angie was gone.

Cam saved the train fare by walking home.

@%&#!!!

There it was, parked outside the fish store: Cam's GTO. Or at least what used to be his GTO. Now it was all fixed up—new paint (silver instead of black), fourteen-inch rally wheels, new rims shining in the sun.

Of course. The bastard didn't just *take* the car, he didn't just *sell* it. No. He had to twist the knife.

And it hurt. A lot.

"Hey!" The knife twister was getting out of the car, hailing Cam like an old friend. "What do you think, man?"

Cam was thinking about getting behind the wheel of the GTO, running over Jerry (and then Hu, for good measure), and driving away as fast as those new rally wheels would take him. So he chose not to answer the question; he just handed Jerry the envelope. Hu emerged from the storefront, stone-faced as always.

Jerry thumbed through the stack of bills. "Uhhhhh . . . there's only two grand here, man. Where's the rest?"

"Give me a few more weeks. I'll get it to you."

"That's past the deadline, Cam."

Hu sidled up to his partner and crossed his arms: the non-verbal equivalent of adding "yeah" to the end of Jerry's sentence. In a way, that was Hu's entire function: being nonverbal.

With difficulty, Cam tore his eyes away from the GTO in all its renewed glory. "I was hoping we could renegotiate. I have a new job. Look, you can raise the vig if you want to. But this is all I can do right now."

"I can raise the vig?" Jerry repeated, as though Cam had said something unbelievably stupid.

Hu continued to be nonverbal and then punched Cam in the gut.

Cam doubled over; he couldn't help it. The guy knew how to deliver a hit that made it seem extremely challenging *not* to hurl. Hu followed up with a choke hold. Next Cam got to check out the car's new paint job close-up, as his face was smashed into the hood.

It was one thing to beat on *him,* but Hu was really crossing the line mistreating the car like this.

"The vig's *already* raised. Go ahead and add another five
percent. You keep acting like I'm the boss, Cam." Jerry put
his head down close to Cam's. "I'm not, all right? Chen is the
boss. The money you owe me, *I owe Chen.* You put me in a
tight spot here." Hu's hold slackened a bit, enough that Cam
could turn his head. Jerry had stepped back a little; he was
smiling down on Cam, pretending to be a concerned friend.
"I don't want to see anything happen to that friend of yours
and her little boy," he said softly. "But if you don't make this
right, it will. Those are the rules."

Hu released Cam, giving him a push as a parting shot.
Cam lay on the sidewalk and watched the two of them drive
away. In his car.

"Two weeks. Get us the money, Cam," Jerry called out
the window.

Cam tried to get up, but he was feeling the combined
effects of the sucker punch and choke hold. For the moment,
he settled for crouching on all fours, coughing as he tried to
regain the ability to breathe.

It was a definite low point, even for him.

He raised his head and looked in the front window of

the fish store. The dark, silent forms of huge, predatory fish swam excitedly through the water of a tank. Through the watery glass, he saw a set of human eyes watching him. The older Chinese lady who worked there—she seemed to always be there—met his gaze.

She blinked at him once, the expression in her black eyes impossible to read, and then calmly finished feeding the fish and walked away from the window.

Cam heaved himself back to vertical and hobbled down the block toward a bodega. He reached into the ice chest outside the store and grabbed a bag of ice, shoving it up against the side of the building to break up the chunks.

His phone vibrated in his pocket. It was Dylan.

"We're going out tonight," he said. "Wanna come?"

"Work?" Cam asked, feeling tired.

"More like play."

Suddenly, Cam felt less tired.

"Where should I meet you?" he asked, already walking toward the subway.

Cam smiled as he stepped off the elevator. He was meeting his friends at a rooftop club in the East Village; the space was filled with torches, and a lot of very pretty girls wearing very little clothing. On a raised platform in one corner, a DJ stood in front of an impressive bank of mixers. The steady thrum of a trance mix filled the air. The speakers were loud enough that Cam could feel the beat through his feet. Dylan caught his eye right away, and Cam strode over to join the group. Everyone but Miller was there, sitting around a big table, drinking and talking.

Cam had almost forgotten about the bruises blooming on his face from his run-in with Jerry and Hu . . . until he saw Nikki's eyes as he sat down.

"Hey." She pointed to her own face. "What happened here?"

So now she cared about him and his face? Cam stared back at her. He was a guy who'd always prided himself on being fast, but even he didn't downshift that quickly.

He tried to make out whether Nikki was wearing the necklace he'd given her, but if she was, it was hidden under the collar of her shirt.

Looking away, Cam lied. "Biffed a wall trick."

Tate snorted. "How's the wall?"

Cam rolled his eyes. He spotted a waitress circling near their table. "Can I have a water?" he asked.

The girl nodded and gave him a wide smile. "Sure thing,

doll." With a wink, she disappeared back toward the bar. Nikki rolled her eyes.

Cam grinned, his mood suddenly lifting a notch.

"I got this on a broken railing," Tate was saying. Cam forced himself to pay attention to Tate as he peeled back his shirtsleeve to reveal a short, jagged scar.

Cam nodded in approval. It did look nasty. "That's nothing," Dylan interjected, pulling up a leg of his pants. "Razor wire."

With a grimace, Cam acknowledged that Dylan's was the worst. "Why don't you show them what happened here?" Nikki was pulling her brother's face around toward Tate, Jax, and Cam. There was a scar there, over his left eye.

Dylan shot her a look, batting her hand away.

"That from a curb?" Cam asked.

Tate laughed. "No. Older lady."

"Hello, Grandma." Jax whistled.

Dylan shook his head and held up a hand. He clearly wanted to be the one to tell the story. "She was a nice Chinese girl—real smart. I met her on the subway . . . whatever, whatever . . . Anyway, I see her walking down the street one night with this guy I assume must be her cousin or something, so I go up to her, give her a big hug and a kiss, and she freaks out, like she's never seen me—goes totally crazy. Turns out, because . . . it was her husband."

"The husband: mixed martial artist," Tate added.

Jax slapped Dylan on the shoulder. "Bad news for the lady-killer here."

Cam laughed. "So is that why we can't cut through Chinatown?"

Dylan shook his head. "Nah, that's all Miller, man. He's got bad blood with the gangs there."

"The Tong?" Cam asked. He didn't miss Nikki's raised eyebrow.

Nodding, Dylan said, "Yeah. Some business went sideways. He had to cut a deal. Promise to stay away."

Nikki wasn't saying anything—not out loud anyway. But her eyes were sure saying a lot. Cam just wished, as usual, that he could figure her out. The waitress came back with his water, brushing his arm as she leaned in (closer than necessary) to hand it to him. Cam turned the full wattage of his grin on the waitress, whose cheeks flushed with pleasure at the attention. He forced himself not to look over at Nikki.

But then he had to look, as Dylan pointed at his sister. "You know, Nikki's got some battle scars."

She frowned and pushed Dylan away. "I don't know what

he's talking about. Not happening." She turned to Cam. "If I showed you, I'd have to kill you."

But for some reason she was actually smiling at him over her beer bottle.

"Don't sling it if you can't take it," Dylan told her.

Jax groaned dramatically, then pointed across the roof. "There she is: the future Mrs. Jackson Smith. Right there."

"Oh yeah?" Cam replied.

"That's gonna be my future wife. Yeah, we're gonna move to the country, make lots of sweet ginger babies every night of the week."

Everyone was laughing, but Jax continued undaunted. "I know. You're jealous." Tate laughed harder, and Jax frowned at the group. "You guys know nothing about women," he said, shaking his head.

Nikki ruffled Jax's hair, then headed toward the dance floor.

Cam slapped Jax on the back. "Hold on to the dream, buddy," he told him.

Tate and Dylan wandered off, and Nikki disappeared, leaving Cam and Jax alone at the table. It soon became clear to Cam that Jax had been drinking more than he'd thought.

"You get it, don't you, Cam?" Jax asked, looking up from

his beer. "I mean, you're right—it is a dream. It's *my* dream," he added in a stubborn voice, as though Cam had been arguing with him. "All that stuff I was saying was true. Even the ginger babies. I wasn't lying. I actually want that. You get it, right?"

"I totally get it, man."

"You want that someday too? Wife? Little Cams jumping off the furniture?"

Cam laughed involuntarily at the image Jax conjured. "Actually that sounds sort of terrifying. Imagine a little kid learning parkour." Cam shuddered. "Imagine the *doctor bills.*"

"You could teach them to be careful. Put lots of mattresses on the floor," Jax said, slurring his words so that the last part came out *math dresses on the four.*

Cam smiled at him. Jax was one of those guys who got all moody and pensive about life when he'd had too much to drink. That was one reason Cam was strictly a water guy these days. If he started down that path, he might never stop. Better to keep compartmentalizing (and stay hydrated, as a bonus).

"We have to get out of this life first," Jax was saying. He raised his blue eyes to meet Cam's. "It's no life for a kid."

Cam thought about Miller's cold eyes and probably

colder heart and wondered how he'd react to a member of his "family" getting distracted by marriage. "You got that part right," he told Jax.

"Maybe someday," Jax said.

Cam lifted his water bottle and held it out to Jax, who, after a few seconds of delay, raised his bottle and accepted the toast. "To someday."

Jax wandered off a few minutes later, having imbibed enough liquid courage to approach his future wife.

Cam stayed. He had a good view of the dance floor from where he sat.

This was important because Nikki was dancing.

And Cam was staring—but she didn't notice. Nikki danced alone, in the center of the floor, moving from firelight to shadow and back, completely oblivious to anyone or anything except the music.

Something felt tight in his chest as he watched her. After a few more minutes of (probably creepy) staring, he realized he'd started walking toward her—not even thinking about it, just moving closer to her, like there wasn't anywhere else he *could* go.

It wasn't long before she sensed him standing near her. Her eyes flew open, locked on his. But she didn't run away.

Cam moved even closer, put his hands on her waist; she kept swaying to the music, her body close to his.

In the flickering light from the torches, there was a tiny flash of silver at Nikki's neck. Cam reached out and slipped two fingers beneath the chain, slowly pulling the tiny bird-cage pendant from where it had rested under her shirt. He let his fingers close around it. The metal was warm from contact with her skin. They were staring into each other's eyes. It was hard to breathe.

He lowered his head; she raised hers. It felt like the most natural thing in the world for him to kiss her. But then she shifted gears, pushing at his chest with one hand.

And running away.

There was a ledge, about three feet tall, between Nikki and the exit. Cam watched her jump up toward the door. The move wasn't very graceful. In fact, she almost fell.

Maybe this wasn't actually a game to her, even though at that moment it sure felt like it.

When he saw her wobbly landing, though, that did it. He took off after her, following her out of the dance area, down the stairs, and out onto the street.

"Hey," he said, reaching out to touch her arm.

She turned around.

"What happened?" he asked, hating how his voice sounded—like he was pleading with her to tell him the truth.

She shook her head. "Nothing. It's just stuffy as hell in there."

Cam saw that she'd hidden the pendant again, beneath the collar of her shirt.

He moved a half step closer, keeping his hand on her arm. "Do you want to get out of here? Go somewhere else?"

"Not right now. I can't." Her words came out clipped. Robotic, almost.

"What's wrong?"

"Nothing, I . . ." Nikki bit her lip, not meeting his eyes.

"Nikki. What are you afraid of?"

The eyes she raised to his seemed too bright. Was she trying to tell him something?

Then she jumped as a motorcycle pulled up close to where they stood.

Miller hopped down from his bike and took off his helmet. "Hey, guys. Sorry I missed the fun," he said, giving Cam a quick one-armed hug. "Had some business to take care of." He turned to Nikki and handed her a helmet he'd grabbed off the back of his bike.

Cam felt the ground shift beneath his feet as he watched her put the helmet on. Suddenly, everything made sense.

And nothing made sense.

"You okay?" Miller asked.

He felt a nervous jolt, then realized Miller was almost certainly talking about the bruises decorating his face. "Yeah. I'm fine." Now *his* voice sounded robotic, but it was the best he could do.

"Hey, Cam—you need anything at all, you call me, all right?"

Cam forced himself to nod. Forced a casual smile.

A casual robot smile.

Cam wished he really were made of metal, just then. That he could turn off the pain that sliced through him the moment he understood what was actually going on.

Miller was still staring at him in that shrewd way of his. After a moment, he straddled his bike.

"Ready to go, Niks?" Miller asked. Cam watched as she climbed on behind him, wrapping her arms around Miller's waist.

Nikki shot him a look before they drove away. It seemed like she felt sorry for him.

That just made it so much worse. Cam stood staring,

long after the bike had disappeared. He realized at some point that Dylan was standing beside him.

"You coming back in?" Dylan asked.

Cam shook his head. "No. I'm tired. I'm gonna hit it."

Dylan nodded, but didn't say anything.

Cam walked the whole way home.

@%&#!!!

TWELVE

IT WAS PROBABLY a mistake for a squatter paying zero rent to blast music outdoors.

But the amount Cam cared just then: zero percent.

He'd been back from the club for maybe two hours. Sleep wasn't even something he bothered to attempt. His head was too full. As he sat on the roof, looking out into the dark, he couldn't stop seeing her climb onto the back of Miller's bike; the moment replayed itself in his mind's eye, over and over.

Now it all made sense: the way she kept pushing him away, all the things she didn't say.

Nikki was with Miller.

Cam felt another wave of anger wash over him. The idea of her being *with* him—as upsetting as it was—wasn't even the worst part. The worst part was the way Nikki had kept on *not* telling him, letting him follow her around like some lovesick parkour puppy. The way he'd invented all kinds of reasons for her reserved, closed-off attitude. Maybe someone had hurt her. Maybe she was getting over something from her past.

Maybe she was shacking up with their boss.

The night was clear, almost cool. It was the end of summer—the perfect season for Led Zeppelin. He sat on the roof, drinking iced tea mixed with lemonade; he closed his eyes and let the bridge of "Stairway to Heaven" wash over him.

The others had to have known, of course. He understood now why the mood had gotten so tense at the guys' loft when the subject of Nikki's "roommate" came up.

It wasn't like he'd tried very hard to hide his interest in her.

Only one good thing had come from watching Nikki climb onto the back of Miller's bike: at least the truth was out now. He could stop trying to figure out her whole hot-and-cold routine, the hundred times she'd bitten her lip, afraid to speak. The way she'd run away from him over and over. It was because she was dating Miller. She lived with him. Maybe she even loved him.

The song ended, and apparently so did the playlist. Cam's phone was lying a few feet away and he heaved himself to his feet to go check on it. That's when he heard the crash. It sounded like it had come from the stairs. Curious, he made his way carefully down through the almost pitch-black stairwell.

He heard swearing.

Rounding the next set of stairs, Cam almost tripped over her.

"Nikki?"

She was still letting loose with a highly colorful series of words. He bent to offer her a hand. She glared up at him and groaned, but then took it.

"What . . . happened?" he asked.

It was hard to tell in the dark, but she seemed to glare even harder at him. "I fell."

"I got that part. How . . . ?"

What he wanted to say was, you jumped off a five-story building the day I met you, and you landed on your feet, so what's with the tripping-*up*-the-stairs routine? But he restrained himself.

She was here. He hated the feeling that was swelling in his chest, because he thought it was probably hope. And he knew from hard experience how dangerous that stuff could be.

Nikki blew a lock of hair out of her face. "Well, if it weren't pitch-black in here, maybe I wouldn't have."

He smiled. "I'll look into having some motion-sensor lights installed," he said. "You know, in this building I'm occupying illegally."

She seemed to realize then that she was still holding on to his arm, and she let go, stumbling slightly but grabbing on to the railing at the last second.

Cam shook his head at her. "And I used to think you were so graceful." When she didn't respond, he changed the subject, keeping his voice neutral. "How did you find me?"

She shrugged. "I wanted to talk to you."

Cam crossed his arms. He felt a spark of anger edging out his happiness at seeing her. The time when he'd wanted—no, *needed*—her to talk to him, that time had passed. He asked the only question that was left between them. "Why didn't you tell me you were with Miller?"

He had the satisfaction of seeing her flinch. "It's not . . . I didn't. Just . . . it's complicated, is the thing."

"Complicated?" he echoed.

"Dylan—he got into some bad trouble a while back. And Miller made it go away."

The spark of anger grew into a fire at her words. So much for trying not to care. "Your brother pimped you out to the boss. Seems pretty simple to me."

She tried to back away from him, but her back was already against the railing. "Miller doesn't own me," she shot back defensively.

Cam stepped closer. "Is that right?" he demanded. "Why are you here, Nikki? What's the point?" With considerable effort, he managed to keep his voice low, because otherwise he'd be shouting at her. He was so mad, he felt almost sick.

"I should've told you. It's my fault. But, Cam . . ." She raised her eyes to his. "You wouldn't be here if I didn't . . . if I hadn't . . ."

"You're right. I wouldn't. So . . . you want me to quit?"

"You can still walk away . . ."

He grabbed her arm. "Is that what you want?"

She looked down again. Her voice was nearly a whisper. "I don't want you to owe Miller like we do . . ."

He felt his grip on her arm tighten, but she didn't pull away. He lowered his face to hers. He spat out each word very precisely: *"Do you want me to go?"*

Nikki shook her head. Finally, she spoke, the word escaping as though it were painful: "No."

Cam closed his eyes. She'd said it—that one small word: *no*. She didn't want him to go. And yet he knew that moving one step closer to her would not, *could not* end well. He'd already made a terrible mess of every part of his life. Why would he take another step toward Nikki and all the trouble she was guaranteed to bring him?

He opened his eyes. There was no reason. This wasn't about reason, and never had been.

So he took that step, closed the small distance between them.

And then he was kissing her, finally. She didn't push him away. She wrapped her arms around his neck, pushed even closer to him, deepening the kiss. A small sound like a sigh escaped her lips. He pulled away for a second, breathing hard, and looked into her eyes. He didn't ask the question out loud, but that moment was her chance to get away.

She didn't take it—she pulled his head down to hers again. He lowered his hands, picking her up, lifting her against the wall. He moaned, low in his throat. Both of them were breathing hard, eyes still locked. She pushed up at the hem of his T-shirt, and he helped her peel it off.

It was still very dark in the stairwell, but his footing was sure as he carried her up to his makeshift bedroom, and they fell together onto his bed.

He laid her down in the tangle of sheets. "Sorry about the mess."

She reached up, ruffling his hair, and smiled crookedly up at him. "I think that's my line."

He smiled, then leaned down to nuzzle her neck. He must have hit a ticklish spot because she giggled.

"Hey, you're kind of ruining the moment for me here," he said, mock-frowning.

She sat up slightly, biting her lower lip and looking up at him through her lashes. "Really? Are you sure?"

His face broke out into a grin. "Nah." He took great pleasure in stopping her from biting that lip by taking over the job himself.

They lay tangled together in his messy bedclothes, listening to music. Nikki surprised him by knowing all the words to his favorite Zeppelin song, "Over the Hills and Far Away."

"You've got a nice voice," he said, lazily tracing his hand in circles over her bare back.

She arched her neck to look back at him. "Thanks. I was the vice president of the chorus in middle school."

Cam raised an eyebrow. "Vice president of the chorus, huh? How sweet. Who knew you were so heavy into school activities?"

She narrowed her eyes at him. "It was seventh grade, Cam. I'm sure you were supercool in seventh grade."

"Baby, I was always cool," he said, lying back and crossing his arms behind his neck. She shifted position, holding herself up on one elbow and peering down to look into his eyes.

"Always cool, huh? How come when I met you, you were biting it on the hood of a cab?"

He sat up abruptly, pushing her away from him. "Maybe because someone jumped off a building and landed *on top of me*." He tackled her then, moving so he was propped up on his elbows, looking down at her. Her hair was spread out over the pillow and he couldn't resist running a hand through it.

"I guess it *was* sort of my fault . . ." She started biting her lip again, driving him crazy.

"*Sort of* your fault?" He tightened his grip on her arms. "Nik . . ." He pretended to glare at her.

"Maybe mostly my fault."

"Uh-huh. Well, tonight it was *you* doing the falling."

"What?"

He grinned. "Do I need to remind you that I found you flat on your butt in my stairwell not two hours ago?"

"I can't believe you're reminding me of that."

"I'm just glad you fell for me." He grinned harder, but stopped when she kicked him. Luckily it was in the shin.

He retaliated by tickling her again, which once more proved highly effective. When she finally gave up and promised no more kicking, he gathered her against him, resting his head on her shoulder.

"I love this song," Nikki said; this time, it was "Kashmir."

"A beautiful girl who loves Zeppelin," he said. "You're never leaving this room."

"It reminds me of home," she told him. "My mom had this old radio, and she used to bring it out on the porch and listen to the classic-rock station. She'd just listen for hours. She said Zeppelin reminded her of summers at the beach."

"Where's home?"

"Very far away," Nikki said. "This little nothing town in Florida." She put a hand on his chest, propped her chin up to look at him. "I never saw a town bigger than, like, five hundred people before I left home."

"Well, you're lucky. All I've ever seen is this jungle."

"You've never been outside the city?"

He sighed. "I don't count my jail time . . . I was going to leave . . . right after my mom died. I found out she still had my dad's old car. She'd had it all along; she never told me. I'm sure she was afraid I'd sell it to help her out. I would have too. So she kept it a secret. She wrote me a letter, said she wanted me to fix it up, get it running again, and go somewhere. Just get in and drive . . . as far away from here as I could get. California, maybe. That was the plan."

"Where's the car now?"

"The bank took it."

"The bank . . ." Nikki frowned at him. "Cam, you can tell me."

"Okay, it wasn't the bank. I do owe money. Just not to the bank."

"I kind of got that part. Who, though? The Tong?"

Cam felt a stab of apprehension go through him. "How did you know that?"

She smiled her crooked smile again. "Lucky guess. Relax. You just seemed oddly knowledgeable about the mob in Chinatown the other night. I put two and two together."

"Uh-huh."

"So you borrowed money to help your mom?"

"Yeah."

"I'm sorry, Cam."

He gathered her closer to him, resting his head on top of hers. "Yeah. Me too."

"So how much do you owe?" she asked, her voice very quiet.

He sighed deeply. "I'm still in for seventy-five hundred."

"What's the interest rate?"

Cam chuckled. "The vig? It varies. Well, it goes *up*. If you don't pay your debt down fast enough. Or if the guy who holds the marker is a jerk . . . which is *definitely* true in this case. Anyway, last I checked, it was up to thirty-five percent."

Nikki sat up. "Thirty-five? Cam! That's twenty-six twenty-five—on top of the principal."

He smiled at her. "Wow, so you're a math whiz too?"

She smiled back, a blush spreading over her cheeks. "I've always been really good with numbers."

"Should have hooked up with you sooner."

"Well, I wouldn't have let you make a deal for thirty-five percent. You might still have your car."

"Guess I'm just one of those people who can't hold on to anything nice."

Nikki nestled in closer to him. "Maybe you just need practice."

THIRTEEN

EVERYTHING WAS PERFECT . . . until the morning. Until he realized it was time for Nikki to go home.

Home, as in where she lived with Miller.

Cam's arms were wrapped around her, and he couldn't make himself let go. "You can't go back there."

"I don't have a choice, Cam. It's where I live."

"Yeah, well. People move every day, Nik."

She sighed. "That's not what I mean and you know it."

"I don't *know* why you need to stay there. Not if you don't . . . feel the same anymore. You don't, do you? Feel . . ." Cam tried to finish the sentence, but couldn't quite manage to get the words out.

Nikki leaned in close to him and kissed him on the cheek.

"I don't. But James is . . . he's not somebody you wanna mess with."

Cam groaned. *James.* He so did not want to know the guy's first name.

More than that, he didn't want to imagine Nikki *saying* his first name. He shook himself, literally, and Nikki frowned.

"Cam. You have to hang in there. Until . . ."

"Until what, Nik? What's gonna change for us, huh?"

She stared at him for a few seconds. "I bought a lottery ticket the other day," she said, trying to smile.

He smiled back, in spite of himself. "Maybe we should hit Atlantic City instead. How are you at counting cards, math whiz?"

"I'll Google it," she promised. Then she kissed him on the cheek and snuggled against him.

They dozed for a little while. Cam was awakened by the sensation of Nikki tracing his infinity tattoo with her fingers. Her voice was sleepy as she asked him, "I heard once that tattoos are scars you give yourself, to show people the pain that's on the inside. Is that true?"

Cam opened his eyes and looked at her. Her hair was a wild, adorable mess. "I don't know. How come you don't have any?"

"'Cause I don't want anybody to know." Her eyes slid away from his.

Cam looked at her. She was always doing that: opening the door, just a crack, then slamming it shut.

"What's this one?" Nikki was searching through his ink and found an image that was almost always hidden. "Is this a *flower*?"

"It's a rose, yes."

"Roses are flowers, smart guy," she shot back, though her voice was playful. "Isn't that kind of girly?"

He sat up, glaring at her. "If you must know, I got that one to impress a girl."

Her eyebrows shot up. "Oh? Do tell."

"You sure you want to hear this story?"

She nodded, but her voice was less certain. "Yeah, tell me."

"She was my first serious girlfriend. Her name was Mel—"

"No names!" Nikki broke in.

"You're the one who wanted to hear the story."

"Yeah, okay, keep going."

"Well . . . *her* favorite movie was *Romeo and Juliet*. You know the one with Leonardo what's-his-name?"

"DiCaprio, yeah."

"Yeah. Anyway, there's this line in *Romeo and Juliet*

about how a rose would smell as sweet as Romeo's name or something. So she talked me into getting it."

Nikki started laughing. "A rose would smell as sweet as his name!" She lay back against the bed, her hand on her stomach. "That's not how it goes. It's 'a rose by any other name would smell as sweet.' It's because their families are enemies, and Juliet's saying that if he were named something else—if he wasn't part of this rival family—he'd still be the guy she loves."

"Oh, well, that's actually sort of romantic," Cam said, nuzzling her neck.

Nikki jumped as the wail of a siren pierced the air just outside the open window.

"Ah, the lovely sounds of summer in the city," she said, clearly trying to steer the conversation back to lighter topics.

"It's the worst," Cam agreed.

"Yeah. But only if you're like us. For people with money, this city's cake, right? They get picked up in a black car—air-con, heat, probably soundproof windows. They get dropped off and picked up, door to door. It's like they float above the surface of the city, you know?"

"You mean guys like Miller? Jax told me he's got a penthouse in the Village."

A strange expression crossed her face, and she rolled away from him. "Miller's not floating. He gets his hands dirty."

Cam closed his eyes. "Yeah, you're right—he doesn't float. I'd say it's more like he slithers." When Nikki didn't respond, he opened his eyes. "You know, like a snake."

"I know what *slither* means. I just don't get why you'd say that."

"I don't trust the guy. Why—do you?"

"He's done a lot for us."

"Guess we'll see. But I get what you mean about this city. Someday, I'm gonna live in a place where you don't need a limo and driver. Somewhere less crowded. My mom's from this little town in Southern California—Lone Pine. I've seen pictures. There's, like, open spaces. Mountains. Trees."

"There are trees in Central Park."

"Not the same thing, Nik."

"What would you do there? In this little town?"

He felt his eyes closing again. "Something with cars, probably. I'd like to be my own boss for once. You know? Maybe sales," he added sleepily. "I can be charming when I want to be."

Nikki rolled her eyes, but she nestled in close to him. "Much *too* charming," she agreed.

The light was streaming in through the curtainless windows, and neither of them drifted back to sleep. Nikki sat up first. "I have to get back."

Cam sat up too. "Will he know? That you were out all night?"

Nikki shook her head. "He had to go to Philly for a deal last night. But he'll be back this afternoon." She pulled the tangled sheet against her chest like she was suddenly feeling shy.

Cam balled up his own corner of the sheet in his fist. It was suddenly hard to speak. "You want me to go back with you? Just back downtown, I mean . . ." His voice trailed off.

She shook her head. "No, Cam. It's not a good idea."

She kissed him quickly—a good-bye.

Without saying anything more, Nikki grabbed her clothes, dressed quickly, then slipped back downstairs.

As Cam lay there, trying not to think about the place she was headed to, her words echoed in his head.

It's not a good idea.

Nikki had been right about Miller being back in town; a few hours after she left, he called Cam about a job, giving him just half an hour before he had to meet the others. Cam pushed everything except the job to the back of his mind. He had to focus; he and Dylan were taking the lead on this one.

Six hours later, Cam and Dylan landed on the roof of the van as it pulled away from the scene of the crime. The job had gone perfectly—apparently Cam was better than he thought at clearing his mind. Moving one after the other, the friends swung through the van's open cargo doors. They each grabbed a door and slammed it shut.

Now, that was a getaway, Cam thought, grinning, lying on the floor of the van. He sat up and saw that Nikki was driving. Miller was in the passenger seat, holding a police scanner; he winked at Cam. Everyone was peeling off their ski masks.

Miller held up the scanner. "All clear. Good job, boys and girls."

"That's what I'm talking about." Tate was high-fiving everyone.

In the driver's seat, Nikki was quiet. She glanced back toward Cam in the rearview. Miller was regarding her in that watchful way of his. The van rolled on through the dark and quiet streets.

A few minutes later, Nikki steered the van into a deserted garage; Miller led the group out onto the street and pulled the garage doors shut, securing them with a padlock.

"Talk later," he said, patting Dylan on the back and nodding to the rest of them.

Cam called out, "What do you mean? What about our money?"

Miller stopped walking. "Payday's next week, Cam. Same as usual."

Cam pressed on. He couldn't stop himself. With Miller standing in front of him, it felt like someone's fist had closed around his heart, and it was squeezing tight. "When's the next gig?"

"Soon." Miller spat the word out. Then he seemed to change his mind and patted Cam on the back, an almost fatherly gesture. "You did a good job. Now get some rest." He turned to get on his bike.

Cam took a step forward. "You don't understand. I need that money."

In a flash, Miller had him on the ground. He'd grabbed Cam's arm, bent it back, and pinned him. It was a practiced move, but not from parkour. Cam knew the move himself, but he hadn't had a chance to practice it in a long time: it was jujitsu. And, judging from the way his arm felt like it was about to snap off, Miller was very good at it.

Great—add hand-to-hand fighting to the long list of skills on *James's* résumé.

"Is there a problem?" Miller asked, his voice low in Cam's ear.

"No. No problem." Cam had done time. He knew when to swallow his pride and wait for a better opening.

Miller paused for a beat, then let go. Cam sat up, rubbing the feeling back into his hand. Stepping back to address the group, Miller announced, "We've got a big score coming next week. We pull it off, it's bonus time. Fifteen—maybe twenty grand each. That work for you guys?"

Miller was asking everyone, but his eyes were on Cam.

"Hell yeah!" Jax cheered, and Cam remembered his conversation with him the other night. He wondered if Jax would use the bonus to go legit.

Cam found himself seriously hoping that he would.

"Sounds good. Hell, sounds *great*," Tate exclaimed.

Miller was still staring at Cam. "How about it, Cam? That work for you?"

He nodded. "Yeah. That works." He might be up on his feet, but it was still time to keep his head down.

Miller nodded and got on his bike. Nikki followed.

Cam stood staring after them, not noticing or caring that Dylan was staring at *him.*

He nearly jumped when Dylan touched his shoulder a moment later. "Come on, man. Let's get some breakfast." It was almost nine o'clock at night, but Cam was getting used to the group's fondness for breakfast at any hour.

Cam followed Dylan like a zombie. It was tough to wrap his head around the fact that he and Nikki had been together only a few short hours ago. As hard as it had been to let her go then, watching her climb on the back of Miller's bike just now was even worse.

Dylan led them down into the subway, and Cam let Jax and Tate—mostly Jax—fill in the silence as they rode a few stops to the diner near Union Square. "This place has the best pancakes," Dylan promised.

The others kept talking about nothing as they ordered (pancakes all around, except for Jax's waffle), and they ate in companionable silence. The food was good—Cam had to admit. He'd been afraid that the scene playing on continuous loop in his head—Nikki going home to Miller's place (and bed)—would prevent him from being able to chew and swallow. But hunger got the best of him, and he put the scene on pause. Compartmentalizing to the rescue, once again. Cam figured his brain probably looked like that Suffolk County evidence locker they'd broken into: a series of locked cages, keeping all the evidence cataloged and separated.

When they finished eating, Tate spent some time flirting with the waitress at the diner's front counter, and Jax curled up in his seat and started to snore.

"Guy can sleep anywhere," Dylan observed. "He's like a giant baby."

"So how did you guys hook up with Miller?" Cam asked. He knew Nikki's version of the story, but he wanted to hear it from her brother.

"Niks and I were living on the streets when we found parkour. We got hooked—I mean, you understand. We were kids with the whole city as our playground. Miller taught us everything we know. Got us off the streets. We'd be nowhere without him." Dylan's voice was fierce.

It seemed pretty clear that Dylan really did feel like they owed the guy their lives.

"Nikki said he took care of some trouble for you."

Dylan gave him a sharp look, then tried to play it cool by taking a sip of soda. But his hand on the cup shook a little, betraying him. "She told you that?" he asked.

"Yeah."

"What *exactly* did she tell you?"

"Just that you got in some trouble and Miller took care of it."

Dylan was staring at him. He looked upset, so Cam tried to smooth things over. "She really cares about you—doesn't want to see you get hurt."

Dylan still hadn't looked away. "Are *you* in some kind of trouble, Cam? Because if you are, and Miller finds out, it's not just your problem. It's trouble for *all* of us. You get that, right?"

Cam nodded.

"And, Cam? Miller always finds out."

Cam met Dylan's gaze. "I'm good."

Dylan stood up from the booth. "Great." He picked the check up from his end of the table and put it down in front of Cam. "This one's on you." He walked out, pulling Tate along with him.

Cam stared at the check for a few minutes, listening to Jax's snores. Eventually it hit him: he could pay the check, or he could get up and walk out. Jax might be on the hook for the money, or he might not be, but it didn't have to matter to Cam. He sighed and threw a pair of twenties down on the table, even though there was no reason to pay . . . no reason to do the right thing or care.

He walked out of the diner and onto the street, one anonymous face among millions. Ever since his mom died, Cam had drifted through this city, rootless, not tethered to anyone or anything. His jobs were all under the table—real jobs that called for a Social Security number and a W-2, those weren't for ex-cons. And it's not like things were getting any better for him. In the past couple of weeks, he'd lost his (rented) home, his (legal) job, his bike—two of them—and his car.

That was why parkour was perfect, he thought, not for the first time. It required nothing but his own body and breath and nerve. Cam didn't have anything else, nothing to care about.

Except now there was her.

It would be so much easier if he didn't care. If he'd been able to be with her last night, satisfy the urge that had been growing inside him since the day they'd first met, then just walk away.

It would be easier if she didn't make him want things: a place to belong, a future.

He heard a crack of thunder, and it started to rain, but

still Cam kept walking. If she lived alone, or with her brother, or some random roommates, he'd have a destination right now. He'd walk over to her place and stand out in the rain if he had to, waiting for her. Like the lovesick fool he was.

His arm still stung where Miller had twisted it a few hours ago. Standing on the street in front of the place Miller shared with Nikki could definitely lead to a lot worse.

Suddenly, Cam didn't care. After all, as he'd just been realizing, he didn't actually have anything left to lose.

A little over an hour later, she found him sitting on the curb outside Miller's swank apartment; he was soaked and shivering. Though it had been a hot day, the temperature had dropped at least twenty degrees. Nikki put her hand in his— she felt so warm after his long wait in the rain.

"Where is he?" Cam didn't let go of her hand, but he didn't move either.

Nikki gave him a small, sad smile. "He's not here, thank God. Told me he'd see me tomorrow night. But, Cam . . . what were you thinking?"

He sighed. "I wasn't." He let her help him to his feet.

She led him up the street to the bus stop. He figured she was going to put him on a bus and wave good-bye, but she paid two fares, not letting go of his hand. She sat in the seat beside him, her head on his shoulder, not seeming to mind that he was soaked. Between the motion of the bus and Nikki's body warm beside him, Cam let himself be rocked gently to sleep.

In the dream, everything was dry and warm—and safe. Nikki was bustling around a kitchen, setting a table, pulling something out of an oven. He smelled roasted chicken, and he sat down at the table. "What's for dinner?" Cam asked dream-Nikki, and she pulled off the lid of the pan.

She smiled down at him, but when he looked in the pan, it wasn't a roast chicken. It was one of the fish from Chinatown—head and all. Cam looked up to ask her why the fish smelled like chicken, but, instead of Nikki, he was staring into the cold, dark eyes of the Chinese woman from the fish store. He woke with a jolt, almost knocking Nikki off the bus seat.

"You okay?" she asked.

He nodded, feeling embarrassed.

"Hell of a dream," she observed. "You were talking."

Cam was too wet, cold, and tired to pretend to be cool. "What did I say?" he asked warily.

She was grinning at him. "You said, 'I hope it's chicken.'"

He closed his eyes. "I'm just really hungry," he said.

The bus lurched to a stop, and Nikki stood up, pulling him along. "Come on. Let's find you some chicken."

One bucket of chicken and a set of dry clothes later, they sat on Cam's rooftop and looked out over the city. He was still shivering a little. He pulled the sleeves of his sweatshirt down to cover his hands, like he remembered doing when he was a kid.

A pigeon landed on the ledge, moving close to Nikki's arm as she lay sprawled with her head on Cam's lap.

"Stupid bird," she said.

"What did he do to you?" Cam asked.

"He's just stupid is all. It offends me."

Cam laughed. "The pigeon *offends* you?"

"His stupidity," Nikki clarified. "I mean, the thing can *fly*. What the hell is it doing *here*?"

"Is this a dis on my neighborhood? I know it's not as fashionable as the West Village," Cam said, referring to Miller's fancy address.

Nikki sat up, rolling her eyes. "I mean the city, loser. He's a bird. Maybe there are reasons to live here if you're a human—like if you have a great job, or if you're obsessed with Broadway shows or museums or something."

"I didn't know you were so anti-bird when I got you that necklace," Cam observed.

"No! I'm not anti . . . I mean, I love the necklace!" Nikki was blushing.

Cam smiled. "Well, as for your pigeon theory, remember: there are *also* tons of people here, all dropping lots of crumbs and scraps. Perfect for birds."

"Yeah. Living on scraps. What a life."

"Well, somehow I make it work," Cam said, but even though he'd meant his voice to be light, the words came out sounding pretty grim. He looked down at the alley below, his mouth set in a line.

Nikki tugged on his arm, trying to get him to face her. "Hey. It's not forever, you know."

He stared into her huge blue eyes. "It's not?" he asked, his voice coming out as a hoarse whisper.

Right away, he knew he'd crossed the line. He saw her pull away from him, saw her eyes slide away from his.

And yet Nikki had been the one to actually say the word *forever*.

She tried her misdirection trick again. "I meant you'll be able to pay back your debt. Miller said this next job . . ."

"Don't."

Her eyes flew up to his. "Don't what?"

"Don't say his name to me. Not here."

Nikki stood up. "I'm sorry . . ."

Cam stood too, reaching out and pulling her back to him. "No. I'm sorry. I just, I . . . *can't* . . ."

"I get it," Nikki said, rising up on her toes to kiss him lightly. "Pit stop. I'll be right back."

Cam sighed and sat back down on the edge of the roof. Trust Nik to run when the conversation turned heavy. In his hand, he noticed the toy GTO his father had given him—he didn't even remember bringing it up here. He stared at the toy for a while, then pulled the photo of his parents out of his pocket and sat, lost in thought.

"You look like your dad," she said, sitting back down beside him.

They talked about their families, and Nikki got a faraway look in her eyes—the one he often noticed when she talked about home. He wondered if she missed Florida, but some instinct told him not to push her on the subject.

He hadn't planned to steer the conversation back to the future, but she seemed to guess his thoughts. His hand closed tight around the toy GTO. Cam raised his head to look at Nikki—she was sitting so close to him, but was still so far out of reach. She put her hand in his.

"You're leaving," she said, in a flat voice. "Aren't you?"

Cam let go of her hand, only to put his arm around her waist and pull her closer. He stared at her for a few seconds. Her eyes were almost silver in the moonlight, and filling up with tears. One blink and she'd be crying. He nodded slowly.

She blinked.

Cam pulled her even closer to him, and lowered his forehead to hers, hearing her breath, as ragged as his own. "Come with me," he whispered.

"I can't . . ." she whispered back, another catch in her voice.

"Don't think. Just . . . come with me."

Nikki pulled a little away from him. She wiped her eyes and opened her mouth to speak—to tell him all the reasons she couldn't leave this place. But before she said the words, he needed to tell her one more thing.

"I know what you're going to say. You're going to tell me your brother needs you, that Miller won't let the two of you—won't let *any* of us—go." Cam pulled her back to him, holding on tight. She didn't push him away. "But, Nikki, I'm telling you. I don't care. I don't care if any of that's true—or if it's all true. Because ever since you fell out of the sky and crashed into my life, the only thing I care about is you. I'm not leaving without *you*."

They both knew that they could never be together, that they'd never find a way out. But Cam told himself it didn't matter.

If everything else in his life had been a lie, she was the truth. The way he felt about this girl, in this moment. *That* was true.

Cam took a deep breath. Then he stood, and offered his hand to her.

She looked up at him, a miserable expression on her face. Cam let his hand fall.

He held the toy GTO out to her. "Hold on to this for me?" he asked.

Nikki nodded, tears in her eyes again. "I will."

It wasn't the promise he wanted, but, as usual, he made do with the scraps.

Nikki stepped into the circle of his arms, and he held on tight, wishing, like always, for more.

He stood up on the roof and watched her walk out of the building. She looked up at him, smiling, but then all of a sudden she was crying. A second later, she disappeared from his sight. He realized she must have come back inside the building, or he'd still be able to see her.

Cam ran down the stairs and met her on the first landing.

She fell into his arms. She really was crying. "It'll be okay," he told her. He ran his hand through her hair and stroked her head.

After a moment, she pulled away from him. "I'm sorry. I don't know what happened. I was fine, and then I looked up at you, and I just had this feeling . . . it hit me so hard. It felt like I was seeing the future."

"Seeing the future?" he teased. "I didn't know you were psychic."

"I'm not." She wiped her eyes with the sleeve of her T-shirt and hit him lightly on the arm. "It just felt so real."

She was still standing close enough that he could tell she was shaking. He put his hands on her shoulders. "What felt real? Tell me."

She shook her head. "No. I'm being stupid."

"Nik." He gave her a look. "After all this, you pretty much have to tell me."

She took a breath and blew it out. "Okay, but it's nothing. I must be like sleep deprived or something. It's just—I looked up at you, and it was like I had this vision or something. Of you. Dead." She bit her lip. "I told you it was stupid," she added in a rush. "I'm going crazy. Just ignore me."

Cam felt a cold chill at her words. Maybe a different

person living a different life could laugh something like that off. But he was behind in his payments to the Tong. And now he was sleeping with his boss's girlfriend.

Maybe Nikki really could see the future.

"Cam? You okay? God, I shouldn't have told you. It was stupid. I don't know where any of that even came from. Everything's going to be okay, I promise."

She moved closer to him, put her arms around his shoulders. He held on to her, still feeling cold.

He was struck by a memory of something his mother had told him once. She had been very practical—she'd never been one to go in for astrology or tarot cards or superstitions of any kind. But once she'd told him a story about a friend of hers who'd left work and rushed home to check on her kids because she'd had a vision that they were in trouble. The woman found the babysitter asleep and a small fire burning in the kitchen.

His mom had told him, "People are psychic when they have to be."

He passed the following day in a fog, missing Nikki, waiting for the next call about a job from Miller or Dylan. When it grew dark again, he sat alone on the roof. It was warmer than last night—clear with no rain. But, despite the warmth of the summer night, he still felt cold.

No matter how hard he tried, he couldn't shake the chill he felt. He kept thinking about Nikki crying, and what she'd seen, standing there looking up at him.

FOURTEEN

CAM FINALLY drifted off to sleep in the early hours of the morning.

After he woke up, he walked out to his spot on the roof, holding the coffee he'd bought at the bodega downstairs, and there was Miller.

"Great view, Cam. I can see all the way into the future from up here."

Cam tried not to react to Miller's cheesy line. The guy might say stupid stuff, like he thought he was starring in some kind of action movie, but Cam's arm still ached from his last reminder that it wasn't smart to mess with Miller.

"How'd you know where to find me?" Cam asked. It wasn't like he'd filled out an application; one of the benefits of working for Miller was no paperwork.

Miller gave him one of his considering looks. "Dylan told me. You staying here wasn't supposed to be some kind of secret, was it?"

Exhaling, Cam struggled to keep his tone light. "This isn't permanent. Anyway, I thought you were all about staying in the moment."

Miller grinned, jumping down from the upper level of the roof to join Cam on his ledge. "You're a good student, Cam. You pay attention. Take direction. And the best part: you get right back up after you fall."

"Story of my life," Cam said. "The falling part, I mean."

Miller gave him a strange look. "Yeah, well, the important part's what you do after you fall, yeah?" He squinted off into the distance for a moment before turning back to face Cam. "Parkour doesn't have any rules, Cam, but there's a natural order to things. A law that even dogs follow." Miller took a step closer to him, his head cocked just a bit to one side—the way he always looked when he was about to make a Really Important Speech. Cam focused on making his Interested Student face.

"There's only one alpha in every pack," Miller told him. "I learned that the hard way when I was younger. In the back of a Chinese restaurant, trying to beg for my life with a gun in my mouth."

Cam swallowed hard. It was the closest he'd come to finding out the reason behind Miller's second rule: stay out of Chinatown. Apparently there was more to the story than a deal that "went sideways," as Dylan had put it. Usually Miller's eyes were strangely empty, but Cam didn't miss the flash of pain that crossed his face when he mentioned his "lesson" in the Chinese restaurant.

Miller took another step closer. "Is there something you need to tell me, Cam?"

Cam forced himself to hold Miller's gaze, keep his voice level. "You asked me before, and I told you. No."

The older man didn't break eye contact. Great, now they were having a staring contest.

Miller's cold brown eyes bored through him. "Well, I'm asking you again. One last time. Man to man. Is there anything going on that I should know about? Anything that could compromise the integrity of this family?"

Family. When he thought about the word applying to Miller and Nikki, he felt sick.

Cam returned Miller's stare for several long seconds. "There's nothing."

Miller finally broke eye contact, his face falling back into that smile that never quite reached his eyes. He looked around the rooftop, putting his hands in his pockets. "You should get a few plants up here. You know, warm the place up."

"Not really a plant guy."

Miller barked a short laugh. "See you tomorrow, Cam. Pickup's at nine thirty A.M. Don't be late."

"Wouldn't think of it," Cam said, taking a long sip of his now-lukewarm coffee. He watched Miller vault his way down to the street.

Cam stood thinking, clutching his paper cup, wondering why Miller had dropped by.

In the end, he decided it didn't matter. The fact was, Miller had control over the only two things Cam wanted— *needed*—in this world: Nikki, and the payoff on this big job. The money that could buy his life back.

As he finished his coffee, he thought about the look on Miller's face as he'd told the story about his younger self, begging for his life in Chinatown with a gun in his mouth.

It was almost like he and Miller were brothers, they had so much in common.

If only, Cam reflected. He was pretty sure his new brother would kill him in a heartbeat if he gave him half a reason.

Or, if Miller found out about the truly excellent reason Cam had *already* given him.

◆ ◆ ◆

It was only 9:10, but Cam was on the street, pacing. He couldn't wait to see Nikki, even though he would have to pretend not to care about her in front of Miller.

The van pulled up seven minutes early and the door slid open. Miller was driving (Alpha Dog at the wheel). As Cam hopped in, he swept his gaze past Tate, Jax, and Dylan. Before he could think better of it, he asked "Where's Nikki?"

Miller shot him a look in the rearview. "Gave her the day off."

Cam felt a cold sweat break out on his forehead, but then he told himself that maybe it would have been weirder *not* to ask where she was.

Oh my God, what the hell is the matter with you? You are actually *turning into a girl.*

"You okay, dude?" Jax asked. "Because you're acting pretty weird."

Cam punched Jax in the shoulder. Hard. "That normal enough for ya?"

Jax let out a pained breath. "Dude! I was just asking."

"Play nice, children," Miller called from the front seat. "Save it for showtime."

The job was across the river, in New Jersey. As the van

moved through the tunnel, Dylan unzipped a big black duffel and began handing out masks. His jaw was set; he didn't meet Cam's eyes.

Cam accepted his mask, but looked down at it with a sick feeling in his gut. He tried to shake it, but that proved impossible as he watched Dylan pull a semiautomatic out of the bag and hand it to Tate.

"We're going in strong?" he heard himself ask. He couldn't shake that queasy feeling that came over him when things started going horrifically wrong.

It was Miller who answered him, his black eyes meeting Cam's in the mirror. "Told you it was big, my friend."

"We're getting a *cut,* man," Jax reminded him, accepting another weapon from Dylan's bag.

The lump in Cam's throat made it hard to swallow. He pushed the words out with difficulty: "I didn't sign up for this." There was a promise he'd made to himself long ago, and it was one he'd never broken. He'd come awfully close to becoming his dad—but he'd never pulled a gun on anyone.

"You wanted in, now you're in," Miller reminded him.

Cam noticed that Dylan was closing the bag. Everyone was carrying *except* him? The sick feeling in his gut suddenly got a whole lot worse.

"Where's my piece?" he asked, keeping his voice low.

"You're carrying the package," Tate answered. "You'll be fine," he added, patting Cam's arm. "We do this all the time. We never shoot these things."

The van slowed as they pulled off the expressway, and came to a stop a few minutes later. Looking out the window, Cam saw they were outside a bank. "We're doing a *bank*?"

"It's an old bank," Dylan said. "New money. Belongs to the BTK now."

"What's the BTK?"

Miller jumped in: "Vietnamese bangers. This is their Laundromat—they keep a big stack on hand. Couple hundred K."

"Money comes out nice and clean," Tate said, grinning.

"How do you know all this?" Cam asked.

"It's my job to know," Miller shot back.

"How are we getting in?"

Dylan grinned. "Through the front door." He nodded toward the Vietnamese guy who was sauntering up to the driver's side of the van.

Miller rolled down the window and nodded at him. The guy was tall and thin, maybe in his mid-twenties. He was wearing skinny jeans and way too much gold jewelry. "Miller," he said. "Tell your boys to make this look good."

Miller nodded. "They'll make it look good. You sell your part."

Skinny Jeans smiled, revealing a smattering of gold teeth. "Trust me."

Miller turned back to his crew. "Okay. Game time, kids."

He stayed behind the wheel as his team filed out of the van.

"Be safe," Miller cautioned. "Stay out of trouble."

Odd choice of words, Cam thought. As much as he disliked guns, he felt vulnerable walking between Dylan and Tate, who were both armed to the teeth.

"Masks on," Dylan barked. They stopped by the side of the building and pulled on their black ski masks. Dylan turned to Cam. "Just use your head and follow my lead."

Cam nodded and started following. The other three backed against the wall, out of sight of the door, so he did the same.

Skinny Jeans hit the intercom button beside the door, then said something in Vietnamese. The door buzzed and clicked open.

Dylan pretended to charge Skinny then, putting a gun to his head, pushing him inside the bank. The guy was a lousy actor—Cam could have sworn he caught him smiling.

Cam's sick feeling was starting to take on a life of its own. He imagined it was some kind of live animal down there in his stomach, maybe one of those spiny fish from the store in Chinatown. The thing was swimming around, stabbing him in the gut, over and over. He was glad he hadn't eaten any breakfast, because he felt a strong urge to hurl.

They burst in on two more BTK bangers, interrupting their chill time. The lobby of the bank had been turned into the gang's hangout. The bangers had been sitting in front of a flat-screen TV. Someone had paused their game of *Halo.*

They took the time to pause their game. That fact bothered Cam. The gut fish swam faster. The two bangers were already on their feet, reaching for their guns. Tate managed to grab the smaller one, hitting the back of his head hard with the barrel of his gun and sending him to his knees.

The larger banger was aiming a Glock at them. He stared at Dylan with dead, black eyes that made Miller's look like the eyes of a warm puppy. "Toss the gun," Dylan yelled.

The big guy didn't even blink.

"I said toss it!" Dylan's voice grew louder.

Cam watched the scene as though from a distance. Dylan's voice seemed to slow and echo through the former bank's lobby. The big guy's face broke out into an awful smile.

At that moment, Cam felt everything begin to slide sideways.

He'd heard his father use that term all his life—slang for when a job went bad—and the official reason for Miller's ban on Chinatown was a deal that had gone *sideways*. But it wasn't until that moment that Cam understood how perfect the word really was. Right now, the four of them were trying to push *forward*, follow the plan, but this giant kid—with his lifeless eyes, three-hundred-pound body, and stoic face—wasn't budging. There was no way to go forward without disarming him. The ground beneath their feet had shifted, and everything was starting to slide.

Cam watched Dylan shift his mask to wipe the sweat from his forehead; to his eyes, it was as if Dylan were moving in slo-mo. Everything took on a terrible clarity: the twisted smile on the big banger's face, the terrified look in Jax's eyes. The carefully paused game of *Halo*.

"On the floor!" Dylan yelled again, but his voice had really started to betray his panic by that point.

"Come *on*!" Jax yelled.

"We gotta move, man," Tate added.

Dylan raised his gun, aimed it at the big guy.

The kid spoke slowly, deliberately. "You're not gonna pull that trigger."

"GET ON THE GODDAMN FLOOR!" Dylan was screaming at the top of his lungs now.

Cam wasn't close enough to hear the kid's response, but he smiled as he said it, and from Dylan's face Cam knew it had been filthy.

Dylan turned to face Cam, his desperation plain. Something in his expression reminded Cam of Nikki, and suddenly everything snapped back to normal speed.

He caught Tate's eye and motioned for him to toss him his piece. Tate understood, and complied. Cam stepped forward and surprised the big guy by cracking him on the head with the butt of Tate's gun. The element of surprise had worked; the kid crumpled.

The others looked shocked. Cam crossed the lobby toward the wall of glass teller windows. The windows were all sealed shut; it was clear the bank had closed for business a long time ago. Dylan and Tate followed Cam, while Jax kept his gun trained on the guys they'd dropped.

The door was locked, and the only way to open it was a keypad. Miller hadn't said anything about a keypad.

They all looked over at Skinny Jeans, but he looked more panicked than anyone. Any trace of a smile was now gone.

"What's the combination?" Cam demanded.

Dylan stalked over and soon had Skinny in a choke hold—this time for real. He echoed Cam's demand.

"I don't have it," Skinny coughed.

Cam kicked at the door, more out of frustration than out of any real hope of opening it. "Screw this," he said, stepping back and looking for another way in. He was sure there had to be one.

Finally, he spotted it. "I can get in," he told Tate, pulling off his mask.

"What the hell are you doing?"

"I can't see anything with this mask on."

Cam took a few steps back to give himself leverage, then vaulted up onto the long counter that ran along the bank of teller windows. He jumped again, pushing off the counter as hard as he could, propelling himself up through the flimsy ceiling tiles and coming down on the other side of the wall. Now he was past the locked door that led from the lobby to the secure part of the bank. He breathed a sigh of relief when he saw the wide metal door of the vault hanging open.

But . . . it was immediately clear that the stacks of cash Miller had promised were nowhere to be found. The inside of the vault was a mess, and Cam made it worse, ripping drawers out of the wall, opening every bag and safe-deposit box. He stalked back out of the vault, scanning the hallways and offices. The whole place was empty except for a few pieces of broken furniture. "There's nothing!" he yelled. "It's empty."

He heard commotion above his head; a few seconds later, Dylan crashed down beside him. "Three more guys just pulled up in an SUV," he said, his voice breathless.

Before Cam could respond, Jax and Tate fell through the ceiling. Cam spared a glance up and saw that, between the four of them, they'd managed to completely trash the ceiling tiles.

"That was a nice trick," Jax told him, trying to smile. They all seemed to be looking to Cam for guidance. Heart pounding, evil fish swimming up a storm in his stomach, Cam looked up and spotted their salvation: an access ladder in the corner leading up into some kind of storage area.

"Come on," he told them.

They scrambled up the metal ladder and into a crawl space, but by that point the chase was on. The BTK bangers who had rolled up were hard on their heels. *No wonder*, Cam thought—the bangers didn't have to jump up through the ceiling; they could just use the access code.

Cam heard shots below. He led the way through the crawl space, and the others followed. He hadn't planned to take over—hadn't expected them to actually listen to him. But taking charge made him feel slightly less panicked. At least he was doing *something*, instead of just letting everything fall apart around him. They crawled as far as they could go, then hurled back down, into a maze of cubicles littered with broken office furniture. Shots kept ringing out, and footsteps pounded behind them.

The four of them kept running as the heist continued to slide sideways, out from under their feet. They clambered out a side window and up onto the roof, one after the other, then jumped the gap that separated the bank from the neighboring building. The next roof was an obstacle course, littered with piles of lumber and construction debris—luckily, that made the roof feel almost like the cargo ship, like home.

Except: when they were training on the cargo ship, no one was chasing them, spraying bullets with their semiautomatic weapons.

They jumped one more gap, and went sprinting across the next roof. Cam's lungs were burning, but he didn't dare stop. The gunfire didn't stop for more than a few seconds at a time. Dylan moved to the front of the group as they crossed the roof and was the first to jump down, spreading his hands out, a nice clean slide down to the street. Cam followed

Dylan's lead. It was almost too far to jump, but they didn't have time to be choosy about their escape route.

Just before he jumped, Cam glanced over his shoulder. Jax was right behind him.

Cam's body hit the pavement, hard. He rolled to soften the impact as much as he could, and to clear the way for Jax. Cam blinked and looked up, waiting for Jax to make the leap from the rooftop.

In the next second, their luck ran out. A spray of gunfire rang out and Jax tumbled over the edge of the building. He wasn't jumping. He was falling.

He was hit.

The moment Jax slammed into the ground, Cam knew he was dead.

Cam froze for a crucial five seconds. He couldn't look away from Jax's blue eyes—an expression of shock and horror fixed on his face, permanently.

Those five seconds stretched into an eternity as Cam remembered Jax's laugh, his soft spot for rescue dogs, the dreams that had brought him to New York.

The dreams that could never come true.

The police car careened around the corner on two wheels and skidded to a stop at the end of the alley. A female cop was already barking at Cam to get on the ground, and Cam wasn't in the mood to argue.

He felt the hot asphalt against his face and closed his eyes, feeling the pinch as the cuffs locked around his hands. There was no point in struggling now. The only thought that gave him comfort was the fact that Nikki hadn't come with them.

Cam struggled to his feet and let the officer lead him to the car without protest.

He understood that it was all over for him.

FIFTEEN

THEY LEFT HIM in the interrogation room for what was probably only ten or fifteen minutes but felt like hours. His mind kept going back to when he was a kid. How he and his friend Dave Sellers, who lived in the building down the block, had always played cops and robbers.

The weird thing was, Cam always wanted to play the cop. Always.

Usually, Dave was fine with it. He was a good head taller than Cam, but probably weighed about the same. He was painfully skinny, like he was growing too fast to keep enough meat on his bones. Cam was more compact, and strong from the martial arts classes his mom struggled to afford.

Dave seemed to like playing the bad guy, pretending to swagger, coming up with a new catchphrase every week, some kind of quip to toss off whenever Cam caught up to him and pinned him to the ground. Cam enjoyed snapping the plastic handcuffs shut, but his favorite part by far had been leading Dave back to the "station house"—really it was the garage Dave's dad rented in the basement of their building. Mr. Sellers had a long, metal shop table in one corner of the garage, and for the game they'd move it away from the wall. Cam would push Dave into the chair, and he'd perch on the little stool, glaring at him from across the table. Then the questioning would begin.

"Where were you on the evening of September seventh?" He'd ask Dave about his whereabouts, his alibis, his criminal affiliations. All the shows Cam's mom loved were cop shows, and Cam had picked up a lot of the lingo. Dave would pretend to squirm sometimes; other times he'd offer up Anthony Moretz from his building to save his own skin.

To become the cop, Cam would always put on a jacket that used to belong to his father—an old, black fake-leather jacket that seemed like something a gritty New York detective would wear. Beneath the jacket, hanging around his neck, Cam wore his shiny toy police badge. His mom had given it to him for Christmas one year. It was his prized possession, once. Cam had loved to feel like one of the good guys.

As he sat alone, waiting for the Newark police to come in and question him in this real-life interrogation room, Cam briefly wondered what had happened to the old badge. Like so much else in his life, it had gotten lost. But he was also pondering a more important question: When had his life gone so wrong? Was it when his mother got sick? Or further back? Maybe the first time he got in a fight at school?

He couldn't figure out which mistake had been the start of it all.

The longer the cops kept him waiting, the more he was tortured by his memories. He thought about when his father left home for the last time. He'd been ten years old.

They hadn't known it would be their last night together. There had been other nights when Cam had known something was wrong—when he'd understood from his mother's crying, from his dad's nervous energy that his father was off to some kind of big "job" in the morning. After one such job, he disappeared for almost a year At first his mom had visited him, somewhere upstate, every week. But then she'd had to get a second job waitressing on the weekends, and she'd stopped going to visit.

Cam experienced the high price of his dad's lifestyle up close, in the tired lines around his mother's eyes, in the sound of her crying after she thought he'd gone to sleep.

And now, here he was, in the exact same boat.

He sat at a metal table, his hands cuffed in front of him. Someone had once put a coat of green paint over the table's black metal, but the paint was chipping all to hell. On TV, the interrogation rooms always seemed cleaner. Reality was so much crappier.

After an eternity of waiting, a tired and almost-bored-looking police detective finally sat down across from him.

"So my partner tells me you're not feeling chatty," the detective said, breaking into Cam's reverie. "How about this: What about your dead buddy? Does he have a name?" He didn't sound terribly invested in finding out Jax's name. In fact, it sounded like the guy was reading from a script. "Might be nice to let his family know where to pick up his remains," he added, stifling a yawn.

"He doesn't have a family." Cam forced the words out. His throat closed. He hadn't cried since he was a little kid, except for the night his mother died. But, at that moment, he felt like crying.

The detective didn't look remotely surprised at his words. Cam guessed that lots of people who ended up like Jax were on their own.

Cam felt a stab somewhere near his heart when he

remembered Jax's goofy smile, and his dream of having a wife and a bunch of little red-haired Jaxes. They had toasted to that dream just a few days ago. He was a good guy, Jax. He didn't deserve what happened to him.

Cam frowned. The thing was, if you'd asked Jax, he probably would have said he already *had* a family—in the form of Miller and the others. Miller, who had failed all of them . . . but no one more than Jax.

The plan had started unraveling the moment they walked in the door. There was no question in Cam's mind that the BTK had known they were coming. They'd let Skinny Jeans inside, but the bangers hadn't seemed shocked that he was playing both sides. Cam's mind kept returning to that paused game of *Halo*—the bangers' lack of surprise. He tried to feel angry, but instead he felt mostly numb. Across from him, the cop was still talking. He forced himself to listen.

"What the hell did you do to get half the BTK chasing you down Clinton Avenue?"

Cam shook his head. "Look. If you had something real to charge me with, you wouldn't be asking." He'd managed to learn a few things, watching all those cop shows with his mom. Toward the end, it had been one of the only things he could do for her. At first, he'd sit beside her on the couch. Later, when she couldn't make it out of bed, he moved the TV into her room. He'd sit with her on the bed and they would try to solve the case along with the detectives. He couldn't remember a time they ever rooted for the bad guys.

She'd never made him feel like he was a bad kid either. Even after he'd been to juvie, his mom never gave up hope that he'd get his life together.

The detective looked mildly surprised at Cam's tone, but someone knocked on the door before he could respond. He heaved himself out of his chair and went out to the hallway. Cam could hear the sounds of talking, but he couldn't make out the words.

A few seconds later, the detective walked back in. "Feds want to talk to you." He gave Cam a smile that seemed to clearly say: *Now you're somebody else's problem.*

The bored detective turned to leave the room again. "Good luck, kid." He sighed. He didn't say the "you're gonna need it" part, but it was implied.

As the detective left, a federal agent came in to take his place.

Cam stared at the floor. "I already told those guys, I'm not saying anything without a lawyer."

As the fed walked around to the other side of the table, Cam looked up at his face for the first time.

And the earth shifted on its axis. Cam felt a physical shock, like one of Hu's blows to the stomach.

"MILLER?"

Cam started to stand, but Miller was already getting in his face, shushing him, talking fast.

"James Hatcher," he said urgently. "DEA." Miller—or whoever the hell he was—was unlocking Cam's cuffs.

"What the . . . ? How . . . ?" Cam sputtered. He was sure his mouth was gaping open like one of those fancy fish they sold in Chinatown. "What the hell is going on?" he spat out, standing.

Miller fixed him with one of those looks of his, punctuating it by placing a hand on the gun he wore on his hip. "Breathe, Cam. We don't have a lot of time."

"Where are Dylan and Tate?"

"Driving home in the van. Should be hitting the tunnel any minute now."

Cam let out a ragged breath. "Do they know?"

"They all know, Cam"

The knowledge hit him like another punch to the gut. Without conscious thought, he fell back into the chair. He was still reeling. It felt like all the air had been sucked out of his body.

He looked around the small interrogation room. "Aren't there mics and cameras in here?" he asked.

Miller grinned. "Not when I don't want there to be. Not when I need to talk to a confidential informant."

Cam put his head in his hands. His brain hurt from the thousand conflicting thoughts that were swirling around all at once. He realized Miller was still talking at him, his words spilling out quickly: "How do you think I run this circus? Miller's the man on the ground . . . shipping and receiving, HR, transpo. Hatcher's upstairs: due diligence, new business, client relations. Neither one gets much sleep, but they work well together."

Cam stared at him. "This whole time, I've been working for a dirty fed."

"Or a clean criminal. Depends where your loyalties lie."

"And what about Jax?" Cam asked. "Where do *your* loyalties lie, Agent Hatcher?"

Miller paused. For a moment, it seemed like his armor was about to crack. "Look, I got bad intel on this one. And Jax is gone. I feel horrible. But that's the past. All we have is the present. And in the present, this department thinks you're one of my CIs. Which means you get to *walk out of here*—with me, under my custody, free and clear."

Cam sat up fast and backed away from him, knocking over the chair. "So they can find my body in a Dumpster tomorrow morning? No thank you."

"I'm not going to hurt you. I need you, Cam."

Cam stood as far away from Miller as he could get. But he didn't say anything, just waited to hear *why* Miller needed him.

"The cops are rousting the whole gang. Someone's going to have to talk themselves out of trouble, and that will lead back to me. It's time to cash out."

"Is this your 'one last score' speech? Save it." Cam had seen this scenario play out in enough shows and movies to know: never a good idea.

"It's an exit plan. It goes down tomorrow. But I can't do it without you."

"*I* need ten grand. Today. Right now. Then we'll talk."

Miller shook his head. "Not going to happen."

"Then I'm not helping you. All right? I'm out."

Cam received another one of Miller's icy stares. "Thing is, Cam, it's not just about you anymore. You're part of a family now, remember? You have to think about the welfare of others."

Moving very slowly and deliberately, Miller placed something on the table between them.

The toy GTO.

Cam swallowed past the sudden, terrible lump in his throat.

He shouldn't have been surprised. Miller was just like Jerry, after all. He'd use any scrap of feeling or humanity in a person, twist it to his own advantage. And that's why those guys always won. Because in the end they didn't give a damn about anybody—they were only about saving their own skin. Oh, and getting paid.

Cam tried to speak, but it wasn't easy. "Where is she?" he managed to ask.

Miller cocked his head to the side, like he was still trying to figure Cam out—even though he'd clearly already managed that feat. "I don't want Nikki mixed up in this anymore. You and I are going to finish it."

Cam felt himself nodding. He'd have promised Miller . . . Hatcher . . . anything at that moment. The rest of it happened like some kind of very bad dream: slow-motion and surreal. Miller steering him through the precinct, DEA badge swinging from his neck, people nodding and saying hello to "Hatcher." Cam kept his head down. He felt sick.

Miller dragged him out the door and down the street, depositing him at the big Newark train station. "You can get the PATH from here. Go home. I'll be in touch. Stay out of trouble." Miller walked away.

As he walked through the door of the station, Cam's phone buzzed in his pocket.

It was a text message from an unknown caller. The text was in all caps: MISSED YOUR DEADLINE. Beside the words, there was a little skull emoticon.

Trust Jerry to be cute while making a very serious threat. As Cam shoved the phone back in his pocket, he felt the wheels of the mini-GTO, and something clicked. He remembered he had more to worry about than his own skin on the Jerry front as well.

He raced to the ticket booth and paced up and down the platform until the train arrived. Even though the train was nearly empty, he didn't sit down. In Manhattan, he made a mad dash from the PATH to the L train. When he finally reached his stop, he started running.

Angie answered the door with a shocked expression on her face, but he pushed past her, looking around, afraid he was too late. "You guys need to get out of the house."

"What?"

Cam kept looking around the small house, his panic rising. When Joey came barreling out of the kitchen, Cam swept him up in a huge hug. "Cam!" Joey exclaimed, smiling. "Thanks for the new board!"

Cam held on tight as Angie struggled to pull her son off him.

"I told you to stay away from us!" she cried.

"Pack a bag. It's time to go."

"What?" Angie's voice shook. "I'm calling the police."

Cam set Joey down, and put his hand on Angie's arm. "Angie, please. That'll just make it worse."

"For you?"

"No . . . look, please just trust me. You have to leave. Right now. It's not safe to stay here. I'll let you know when you can come back. I promise." He handed her the disposable phone he'd bought at the bodega on the corner. It had been a long train ride, and he'd had some time to plan.

Angie took the phone, then stood staring at him for a long moment before nodding once. "Joey, get your backpack."

"I'll call you at that number when it's clear. And . . . Angie . . . I *will* call. I'm so sorry."

Joey was tripping down the stairs, holding an open backpack. "Is Cam coming?"

Angie turned to Cam, anger and tears at war in her face. "Fix this," she told him, opening her front door and pushing him out.

Cam walked down the street, his tread slower now. All the adrenaline that had driven him to Angie's door was now gone.

He took the toy car out of his pocket and threw it on the ground, watching the small front wheels break off. He kicked what was left of it into the street.

There was only one thought in his head, chasing around on repeat: some broken things can never be fixed.

SIXTEEN

CAM WALKED ALONE for hours. His mind replayed a series of awful moments on an endless loop: the look of horror on Jax's face as he fell, Jax's lifeless eyes as his body lay on the pavement, Miller standing over Cam with his DEA badge swinging around his neck . . . Miller setting the toy GTO on the metal table between them, a wordless, sickening promise.

There was no longer any question. Miller knew. He knew, and he was turning the situation to his advantage—using Cam's feelings for Nikki to control him, bring him to heel.

Cam realized he'd been wrong about Miller—he wasn't a snake. Miller himself had told Cam what he was: a stray dog—one that had fought its way up from the bottom to become the leader. It seemed pretty clear that this alpha would do whatever it took to stay on top, even if it meant sacrificing the rest of the pack.

Miller had revealed too much, the day before on Cam's rooftop. The flash of pain—and something else (Cam thought it was probably shame)—that was the only moment of true emotion the older man had ever let slip past his defenses. Cam's own dealings with the Tong made it all too easy to imagine what a young boy at their mercy must have suffered.

Cam kicked a beer can that lay in his path. He didn't want to feel sorry for Miller. He didn't want to feel anything but hate for the man who had betrayed him. To make matters worse, everyone else in the group had known that Miller was actually a fed—everyone.

Nikki had known. The feeling of betrayal hit him again like a wave of nausea as he reminded himself that they had all kept him in the dark. He'd come upon a small park during his walk. There didn't seem to be anyone else around. Cam sank down heavily onto one of the benches.

Why had she kept Miller's secret? Was it because she cared about him—wanted to protect him?

Her betrayal hurt . . . a lot. But Cam knew he couldn't let himself off the hook for everything that had happened. He'd been stupid—and greedy. Even though he'd only wanted the money so he could buy back his freedom, Cam could see now that he'd been blinded by greed.

Or maybe that was a lie too, and it was love that had blinded him all this time. Maybe it really was all Nikki's fault.

Suddenly Cam felt an overwhelming urge to see Nikki, to confront her. No matter how not-smart it might be, he needed to find her. She'd lied to him, over and over.

He needed to know why.

Cam sat without moving for hours. He was afraid to go back to his crash spot. And he didn't have anywhere else to go. After his legs grew stiff, and his stomach started growling, he stood up on shaky legs. He bought a gyro from a street vendor and ate it quickly, without tasting it. He took the train to Miller's neighborhood as darkness started to fall. He looked around him; this area was unlike any part of the city that Cam had ever lived in—or spent any time in. Sure, he'd made deliveries on quiet, clean streets like this one, but he'd only ever slowed down enough to hand over the package and get the signature. He thought back to Nikki's comment about the way some people floated over the grimy surface of the city, protected from the dirt and the noise.

He sat on the marble steps of a brownstone down the block; he could see Miller's door, but he was mostly hidden by a Hummer parked on the street. As long as the owner didn't come out and move it, Cam could stake out Miller's place for as long as it took.

Maybe forty minutes after he'd arrived, Cam watched Miller emerge onto the street, taking the steps two at a time and walking briskly toward the subway.

Cam sat staring at the immaculate façade of Miller's building for a few minutes. Apparently the guy's double life had its rewards.

And Nikki was one of them.

Was *this* why she stayed with him? A nice life in the city, cushioned by the money from Miller's thievery?

He needed to understand the hold Miller had over her. But he couldn't just climb those steps and find out if she was still inside his perfect apartment. Miller might come back, or he might have somebody watching the place.

No, he had to smoke her out.

Cam pulled his phone out of his pocket and started texting: i'm here. come outside. Then he hit the backspace key until the message disappeared. It would be just as stupid to meet her anywhere around here. He started typing again:

meet me at 517 walker street. 20 minutes. if you're not there i'm coming to miller's.

It only took about thirty seconds for her to text back: ok c u in 20.

Cam grabbed Nikki's arm as she walked into the nearly empty Laundromat. A few of the machines were running, and a middle-aged woman sat waiting, wearing headphones, her eyes closed. The attendant sat behind a counter in the back, his eyes glued to a small television set.

"Cam!" she yelped, pulling away from him. "You're hurting me!"

He let go. So much had happened—so much had changed—since he'd last seen her. Now that she was so close to him, the feelings of hurt and betrayal hit him in a fresh wave. Actually, *betrayal* wasn't a strong enough word for it.

Her lying had hurt him more than anybody had ever hurt him.

Cam led her past an empty row of washing machines. After staring at her for a few more seconds, he finally managed to ask the question: "Why didn't you tell me?"

Some detached part of him noticed that his voice sounded nearly as miserable as he felt. He was so tired, wound so tight. He felt as though he were standing apart from himself, watching, like this was a story he'd heard, or a movie he was watching late at night, with his eyes only half open.

If only.

Nikki was staring back at him, her eyes washed silver in the dim light. "I tried to warn you," she finally said, in a small, unsteady voice.

Cam laughed, and it sounded pretty bitter even to his own ears. "Yeah, that was a great scene," he told her. "You seemed so broken up about it." He moved very close to her, so close he could feel her breath on his face. "Were you playing me from the start?"

"No!"

She tried to move away from him but he reached out for her again. "No? Really? That stupid bike. That was all a lie, wasn't it? A setup."

"No, I swear . . ."

Cam ignored her, like she hadn't spoken at all. "You guys must have had a great laugh about that. On the ship. All of you who *knew* what you'd signed up for." He lowered his head so that his lips were close to her ear. "You *knew* he was a fed. All this time. You all knew," he hissed, then pushed her away.

"Cam, that bike . . . that was all me. I felt bad about wrecking you out. I wanted to make it right." She took a deep, ragged breath. A single tear rolled down her face, but she didn't wipe it away. "I never thought any of this would happen."

"What *did* you think would happen, Nikki? The guys would just play cops and robbers with real guns and no one would ever get hurt?"

"No—Cam, that's not how . . . *you* wanted in . . ."

He laughed again, and scrubbed his hand over the back of his head. Then he looked into her eyes and dropped his hand to his side, all his lying bravado gone. "No. I wanted *you.*"

Nikki exhaled; she looked like he'd just punched her. He had the urge to laugh again. Or maybe cry.

They stared at each other for a long moment. Another middle-aged lady walked toward them, carrying a basket of clothes. She stopped short when she saw them, an embarrassed look on her face. She turned back and went down the next row of washers. Cam heard the clink of quarters in the machine, then the rushing sound of water.

Neither of them spoke, and the seconds ticked on. Finally, Nikki broke the silence, taking a small step closer to him: "I'm sorry. I wanted to tell you. I did. But I couldn't . . ."

"Why not?"

"Dylan . . ."

"You're *not* blaming Dylan." Cam's voice came out higher than normal.

"No—I'm not blaming . . . it's just, it's *because* of Dylan . . ."

"You mean how Miller bailed him out of trouble. What did Dylan do that was so bad?"

Nikki wrapped her arms around herself, moving away from him until her back was touching one of the machines. "What difference does it make?"

"Tell me. I think you owe me that much."

She nodded, and a few more tears made tracks down her face. "It was bad, Cam."

"Did he kill somebody?"

"I don't want to talk about it."

"I'm sorry, Nikki, but that's not good enough." He stepped closer, and though she seemed to flinch, she didn't back away. "He's your *older* brother, Nikki. Let him take care of his own problems."

A sob escaped her, and then the whole story came tumbling out. She was speaking fast, not quite meeting his eyes. "Somebody did something to me, okay? Back in Florida. And Dylan came in while it was happening. He stopped the guy . . . and then he beat him. Put him in a coma. We had to run . . . but it followed us here . . . then Miller made it all go away." She raised her eyes to his again.

"If this guy . . . attacked you, why were you the ones who had to run?"

"It just . . . it's complicated."

Cam ran a hand through his hair and stepped back, resting against the wall of the Laundromat. He spoke slowly, not wanting her to burst out into any more of those gut-wrenching sobs. "Nik, I get that this is . . . really hard to talk about. And I'm sorry. But you've lied to me—over and over. If you're not willing to be honest with me now, after everything . . . I just don't . . . I can't . . ."

She raised a hand up, slowly, as though to stop him from saying anything more. "Okay. I'll explain. I just—it's hard. I haven't talked about it to anybody, not since it happened."

Nikki took a deep breath. Her eyes were focused on the wall behind him, as though she couldn't bear to meet his gaze. "This guy—the one who . . . I *knew* him. Remember how I told you I used to do gymnastics? So I was good enough that a gym teacher at my school found me a scholarship to this fancy private school. It's not like my mom could have afforded to send me there otherwise. But anyway, that's how I knew him. He competed on the parallel bars—he was really good, was even going to try out for the Olympics." She closed her eyes and added in a smaller voice, "He was really strong."

She exhaled, opened her eyes again. "When he first asked me out, I was—I don't know—flattered? He was really good-looking, smart, and his dad was a *really* big deal. You've heard of him—he's been in like a hundred movies. That's why the mess followed us all the way up here. His dad has a lot of money, and a lot of influence. So I thought, I *should* be crazy about this guy. And my mom was all about him. He was my ticket out of that crappy town, that's what she thought. She was so excited about the idea, of me and him."

She took another ragged breath. "I went out with him a couple of times. But no matter how perfect he was supposed to be, I couldn't get past this feeling I had whenever I was with him. He almost made my skin crawl. I should have broken it off with him right away . . . I guess after all those dates, all those times he bought me dinner and flowers, he seemed to think I owed him. He came to pick me up one night. Nobody else was home. I tried to break it off, let him down easy. But he wasn't having it." Her voice took on a detached quality as she recited the rest, as though the details weren't quite real for her. "He was really strong, like I said. He carried me into my room, held me down . . ." Another sob broke through.

"Stop—you don't have to tell me the rest." Cam struggled

to get the words out. It felt like someone had forced sand-paper down his throat.

"That's when Dylan came home," she finished. "Cam, Dylan was protecting *me* that night. Now I'm protecting him."

Cam's insides were hollow. There weren't any words that seemed right after the story she'd just told.

"That night is why I don't trust myself, Cam. I was stupid, and blind—and I should have been more careful." She was crying harder now. "So, ever since then, I've tried so hard to be. And then you showed up." Her eyes met his. "I didn't mean for any of this to happen. I tried to warn you—tried to forget about you. But I couldn't. When it really mattered, I messed up—again. I'm so sorry it all went down this way, Cam. I never thought you'd get pulled into it. I was scared to tell you anything else because . . . I didn't want you to go. And now it's all messed up and I don't know what to do."

Cam stepped forward and pulled her into his arms. He didn't have any answers, but at that moment it felt good just to hold her.

"I'm so sorry that happened to you," he said. "But you have to know it wasn't your fault. That guy . . ." He felt the anger twist in his gut. He would have liked ten minutes alone with him. "Nikki, *that* guy's to blame. He's the one who hurt you. Just thank God Dylan came home when he did."

"Sometimes I wonder what would have happened if he hadn't. Dylan gave up his whole life for me. He was doing okay back home. When we came here, we had nothing."

"It must have been hard. Leaving your mom."

Something flashed in Nikki's eyes. "It was for Dylan. They're still really close. But she was . . . angry with me. For screwing everything up. She thought I had a chance to be . . . more, to have more, and I just threw it away."

"You know she's wrong, right? That's pretty messed up."

A fresh sob broke from her. "I know. It still hurts, though, you know?"

At that moment, Cam felt himself begin to forgive her. Her own mother hadn't even been there for her. No wonder she was so protective of Dylan, who *had* been.

And he was starting to see why she might be reluctant to tell a powerful, rich man *no*. Another rich man who could ruin her brother's life, take away everything.

He pulled away and looked at her. "Nikki. Do you want to leave Miller?"

She didn't answer. He felt like a cold hand was squeezing his heart.

He stepped away from her. That was his answer. Maybe there was no coming back from the chain of events that had started that terrible day in Florida.

Nikki put a hand on his arm. "I'm afraid to want . . ." she whispered.

Cam lowered his head to rest against hers. Then slowly, very cautiously, he found her lips. The kiss started out careful, gentle, but soon she was clutching at his arms, her need matching his.

He hated what he had to do next. Again moving gently and slowly, he pushed her away and rested his hands on her shoulders. "Go home," he told her. When she looked wounded by his words, he added an explanation: "We can't do anything to spook Miller tonight. You have to go home."

He didn't tell her the other reason he was sending her back to Miller. If the Tong had noticed his attachment to Nikki, it was actually a very good idea for her to stay close to a DEA agent.

After all, Miller wasn't the only one they needed to be afraid of.

Nikki stared at him for a few more seconds. "I don't have a home," she told him.

Cam pulled her hard against him again, buried his face in her hair. "I know. But we *will*," he promised, his voice fierce.

He pushed her a little, out into the night, back toward Miller, the cold hand closing even tighter around his heart.

At that moment, Cam was pretty sure he couldn't sink any lower. He was now exactly 100 percent like his father.

A petty crook who made promises he could probably never keep.

SEVENTEEN

CAM SAT ALONE on a roof a few blocks from the Laundromat. Even though he'd left her hours ago, he couldn't stop thinking about Nikki's story. He'd seen it all unfold in his mind's eye, unfortunately—and it kept replaying on a loop in his head. He felt angry, and powerless. Cam didn't even know the guy's name. There was nothing he could do.

There was no undoing that day—that one day that had changed Nikki. Probably it had defined her.

One day could do that. He remembered his own. The first time he'd broken the law. The first time he'd started down the path his father had laid out for him—the one he'd promised himself he'd never follow.

But then he'd found out about his mom's diagnosis. So

much anger had been coursing through him. He couldn't drink it away. No matter how many fights he picked—win or lose—he couldn't get past it. So when his friend Adrian from his old neighborhood in Queens had shown up with a job, Cam said yes. He'd said no to his old friend dozens of times. But not that day.

They drove all the way out to Elizabeth, New Jersey, in Adrian's old Mustang. The target he'd picked was a sandwich shop in a crappy strip mall. Adrian said he knew the alarm code. Cam hadn't asked how he knew.

The only thought he'd allowed himself as they crouched in the dark outside the shop was that if he came home with some money, then at least his poor mother would have one less thing to worry about that week.

The job had gone off without a hitch. The code worked, they crept in, found the safe in the back. It was one of those cheap ones they have in hotel rooms, where you can pass a credit card through the slot to open it. The card Adrian mysteriously produced worked to open the safe. Cam kept lookout while his friend emptied it.

On the way home, Cam asked Adrian about the code, and the card. His friend told him casually that the shop was his uncle's.

The sick feeling that had come over him then was one he'd never forget. That moment was burned into his memory. But it hadn't stopped him from pulling the next job (though he never said yes to Adrian again). His mother was still sick; they needed money.

Once you've helped some loser steal from his own family, what was the point in even trying to be a better person? That had been his logic back then. It got even worse when he was sent away, and couldn't help his mom—couldn't even be there for her. He got used to living with the shame. Until finally his mom forced him to face his shame head-on—and start to let it go.

It had been in her final weeks. She was so weak she couldn't leave her bed. He fell asleep in the chair beside her, which had started to become a habit. When he woke up, he found her studying his face in the dark. "You need anything?" he asked her.

"I'm fine," she told him. She was lying, of course. She wasn't even close to fine. But he knew she never wanted him to worry.

"You've done things you're not proud of," she whispered, without preamble. They hadn't done much talking about the "career" he'd been pursuing for the past couple of years, since she'd started to get sick.

He met her eyes. It was the middle of the night and he was too tired to lie. "Yes."

"You have to forgive yourself," she told him.

He held her unblinking gaze, then looked away first. He focused on a loose thread in her bedspread while he spoke. "Thanks for that, Ma. But I don't deserve to be let off the hook for anything."

"Don't you? I know why you did what you did."

He looked back up at her. "You do?"

She nodded. "To help us. To help me. That's why you have to forgive yourself."

He was shaking his head before she even finished speaking. "It's a nice thought," he admitted, "but I'm not sure it was as noble as you make it seem." One particular incident when he'd boosted a car came to mind—a Mustang he'd stolen as much for the rush as for the money. There was no way to blame that bad choice on her.

"Of course it wasn't noble. I'm not a fool, Cameron." She smiled gently to take the sting out of her words. "But it started out that way. And that's enough reason for you to let it go. Choose a new path."

He picked at the thread, wrapping it around his finger, cutting off the circulation. Fighting back tears. "It's not that easy. I've got a record now."

"I never said it would be easy. But it's my dying wish. I wouldn't waste it on something easy."

His eyes had flown up to meet hers. "Don't say that!" He heard the panic in his voice. She was all he had.

She smiled at him again. "I wish I didn't have to, baby. But there's no getting out of it. I have to tell you now—make you understand. We all screw up. Make bad choices. They don't have to define you forever."

"You never made any bad choices."

"Ha! I married your father. He was different when we first met. But he changed—he started down a different road. That's what happened to you too, son. That's why *you* have to pick a new road, Cam. You have to promise me."

"I promise."

He hugged her then. She felt so small and light, as though a part of her was already gone. She only lasted a few more days.

He'd kept his promise to her for two years. He'd found a legit job, kept his nose clean. Until he'd fallen behind in his payments to the Tong. Until they started threatening Angie and Joey. Until Nikki showed up.

His mother had been right about starting down a road— and how hard it was to change direction.

Cam looked up at the cloudy night sky and silently made his mother another promise. He'd find his way back to the right road somehow. If she was up there looking down at him, he wanted her to be proud of him.

Finally, Cam reached the point where he couldn't sit anymore, just waiting for Miller to contact him. It could happen at any moment, or it could be hours away.

He didn't dare go back to his new place, and he sure as hell needed to avoid Chinatown.

Nikki was (hopefully) safe at Miller's, and if he'd believed in praying, he'd have asked to be sure Angie and Joey were okay too.

There was no one else for him to protect or worry about, and nowhere else to go.

He started walking again, this time saying good-bye to the city. Because one way or another, it was going to be good-bye.

Cam thought about how his mom always used to get on him for negative thinking. She'd tell him he had to ask for what he wanted. Think positive.

But another part of him knew he was just being practical. He wasn't sure what Miller was planning, but if his "exit plan" went sideways, Cam would be headed upstate, or he'd be dead. And if it didn't . . . well, then he could actually keep the promise he'd made to Nikki and help her escape with him, find a new home for the two of them somewhere else.

Cam stayed away from Lafayette Messenger, and the fish store where Jerry and Hu hung out, but he wouldn't miss either of those places.

He started his tour at Seward Park, where he'd taken his first clumsy stabs at parkour. Then he took the train out to Elmhurst, and said good-bye to the street he'd lived on as a boy, imagined the GTO, in its former faded glory, parked in its old spot on the street. He remembered how his dad had taught him to drive it long before he was sixteen. He'd thought his dad was putting such trust in him, but then his mom explained that his dad didn't like having to wake up early to move the car on days when the street sweepers were coming through. Cam might have been the youngest kid in Queens to master parallel parking. Or maybe lots of dads were too lazy to wake up to move their cars.

As he gazed at his childhood home, Cam realized that he didn't know much about how a regular—a *real*—family was supposed to work. His dad had never been around consistently. Before she got sick, his mom had worked two, sometimes three jobs, just to pay the rent and keep them fed.

There had to be a better way to live, somewhere. Cam started running, attacking every obstacle in his path. Jumping over cars, doing tic-tacs off the sides of buildings.

His heart felt bigger, all of a sudden. He felt alive.

It was one of the first lessons he'd learned: in tracing, you didn't need *anything*—no special gear, nothing that money could buy.

Just your head and body and heart. Just the breath in your lungs. You didn't even really need shoes.

He knew in his bones he was leaving this city, his city, tomorrow, one way or another. A place he hated and loved at the same time.

And it *was* a giant playground. That was the part he knew he'd actually miss.

The first light of dawn was creeping in around the edges of the city, and Cam kept running.

EIGHTEEN

THE CALL came at seven thirty the next morning. Cam got the address from Miller and made his way to the pickup spot. He started pacing the length of the corner where he waited, too full of pent-up energy to stand still.

It was incredibly stupid but the theme from *Rocky* kept playing in his head.

Whatever worked, he figured. Because he knew today was make-or-break. He couldn't control most of it, but he could stay in the moment and, if his shot came, he would take it.

The usual van pulled up in front of him, and he opened the side door. Nikki was sitting in the passenger seat. Tate was driving, for a change. Dylan and Miller were in the back.

Jax's absence was like an open wound. No one said much.

"Where are we going?" Cam finally asked, looking down at the huge duffels filling the entire back of the van.

"We've got a plane to catch as soon as we're finished. This job's in and out. Then we're gone for good."

Cam didn't ask who was included in Miller's *we*. The key point was who *wasn't* included: Cam. Nikki caught his eye, but quickly looked away.

"We'll drop you on the way to the airport," Miller told him. He paused and smiled that empty smile of his. "After you get your ten grand, of course."

"Of course," Cam said, keeping his voice completely flat. He felt detached. He was reciting the expected lines—the expected lies. He and Miller were playing their parts, like actors in a horrible, deadly play.

Dylan handed him a pair of coveralls, like a repair guy might wear. "Put those on," Miller directed. Cam saw that Dylan, Tate, and Miller were wearing the same outfit.

They drove in silence for a few minutes until they reached their destination. The van stopped on a quiet street near Astor Place, in front of an expensive-looking brick apartment building. Again, Cam was reminded of what Nikki had said about the people in this city who were driven from door to door, living in a world where everything was new and neat and clean. This seemed like the kind of place where those people lived.

Cam forced himself to tune in to what Miller was saying. He had to focus, today of all days. "Tate and Nikki are pulling lookout," Miller said. "Me and Cam are making the pickup."

Cam let himself look at Nikki once more on the way out of the van. She looked scared, almost sick. Miller slid the van door shut, and tapped on the side. Tate drove away.

Cam tried not to let himself think about the possibility that he might never see her again.

Dylan went first up the fire escape on the side of the building, Cam went next, and Miller brought up the rear.

When they reached the roof, Miller walked to the center and pointed out the skylight of the penthouse unit just below them. "Where are we?" Cam asked.

"Safe house. The Russians put their VIPs here when they visit." He smiled his oily smile. "They stash other things here too." He wagged his eyebrows suggestively, as if the group wouldn't have gotten his point without the theatrics. Cam groaned inwardly. He was starting to actively hate Miller— and not even just because of Nikki.

"What do you need me for?"

"It's a two-man job," Miller answered.

"Why isn't Dylan going in with you?"

"Dylan's watching our exit." Cam felt like he'd heard Miller's voice harden as he'd shared that last part.

Dylan shot Cam a strange look, then busied himself looking for something in his pack.

Inside Cam's head, the *Rocky* theme had faded out, replaced by a sort of dull roar. Maybe it was the sound of fear.

"How are we getting in? Through the skylight?"

Miller nodded. "Copy that."

"But what's *inside*?" Cam pressed.

Miller's smile widened. "Thought you'd have already guessed, Cam. You've proven such a tracing prodigy. Student has nearly surpassed the master. Down there, *that's* a new plateau."

With those words, Miller handed Cam a gun.

"I don't really know what I'm doing with this," Cam told him, trying to raise his voice over the roaring sound that suddenly seemed to clog his ears.

"It's not loaded."

"You want to drop me in there . . . with an *unloaded* gun? No way."

"I'm going in with you. It's you and me together this time."

Cam gave Dylan a hard look. "You really down with this, Dylan?"

"How about you just do your job, all right?" Dylan snapped, still not meeting his eyes.

Miller grabbed Cam's arm. "Get your head in the game, Cam. Right now. We're doing this for *Nikki*, remember?"

Miller pulled on his mask—Cam recognized it as the one he'd worn for Cam's initiation into the group. He wondered briefly where he'd be at this moment if he hadn't passed. Maybe dead in the trunk of the GTO.

That was the great thing about his life: it full of *almost*-comforting thoughts. Rock/hard place: it wasn't like either of the choices had been all that attractive.

"Let's go," Miller said, his voice muffled by the mask. "Once we're inside, just do everything I say, okay? I've got this all worked out."

The skylight was massive, maybe six feet on each side. Cam risked a glance down at the scene below. The décor was garish—the room was filled with heavy, ornate furniture, and the carpet appeared to be leopard print. He could make out a few people lying on a sectional sofa, possibly watching television. Whoever they were, they clearly didn't know there were uninvited guests about to crash in on them.

"On three, okay?" Beside him, Miller got ready to jump. He rolled up on the balls of his feet. Cam did likewise—he leapt up, and hit the glass with enough force to break it.

Cam crashed through, huge chunks of glass raining down beside him. He landed in a crouch, but he didn't dare roll onto the broken glass. He already felt a wet heat on his left upper arm; he knew he was cut. He didn't stop to find out how bad.

A woman stood up from the couch and started screaming the moment he broke through the skylight. The noise and confusion gave Cam a few seconds to retrieve the gun from his waistband and level it toward the people he'd surprised. There were two men in rumpled suits and two heavily made-up women wearing very tight dresses.

The next moment, Cam experienced a surprise of his own. He realized he was standing there alone.

Miller hadn't jumped.

"Be quiet. Don't move!" Cam yelled, brandishing his unloaded gun with as much fake confidence as he could muster. The screaming woman was still on her feet, and for some reason she took a step toward him.

"Sit down!" Cam told her. A shot rang out behind him, and he heard the thud of a body hitting the floor. Keeping his gun as steady as his shaking hands could manage, Cam glanced back, then up. Miller had shot the man who'd been coming up behind him. He'd been a big guy—probably a bodyguard.

Miller hadn't had any trouble dropping the guy from his safe spot on the roof.

At that moment, Cam understood.

He'd been sent in as bait.

Just as Cam was processing this fact, Miller jumped down and landed a few feet from him. He seemed to land with his AK-47 raised and at the ready. And why not? Cam had already done the hard part and broken through the glass.

"What's going on?" Cam demanded.

Miller nodded toward the crying woman and her friends. "Watch them."

Cam kept his (freaking *unloaded*) gun trained on the two men in rumpled suits. One of them backhanded the screaming woman, and she fell silent. Cam took a step forward, feeling helpless. At least the woman had stopped shrieking.

Miller was behind him; Cam backed up so he was still facing the people on the sofa, but could see Miller too.

Cam saw that Miller was crouching in front of a safe, turning the dial. After a few seconds, he started stuffing stacks of cash into his bag. His movements became slower and more careful as he pulled a small velvet pouch out of the safe.

And then Miller broke one of his own rules: right there in the middle of the heist, he looked inside the bag.

Whatever he saw inside made the bastard smile.

As usual, Cam didn't care what was in the bag. At that moment, all he cared about was finding a way out. "What's the exit plan?" he shouted at Miller.

Miller stood up. Instead of answering, he stalked forward a few paces until he stood beside Cam, just a few feet away. Methodically, in a line from left to right, he shot each of the four people Cam had been guarding.

"This is the exit plan, Cam."

Still calm, like he was ordering a coffee or reading a newspaper, Miller began to change the magazine on the AK. When he was done, he trained the weapon on Cam.

"This was always the plan," Cam said. "The unloaded gun. The jump you didn't make." He didn't necessarily expect his words to change the outcome of the situation, but he wanted Miller to know he understood, at least. Bad enough to be the bait—worse to be a complete chump too.

Miller's only response was a smile.

The moment seemed to stretch as Cam stared back at him. It wasn't that the betrayal was a compete shock. He knew Miller was responding to what he perceived as Cam's own betrayal with Nikki. He knew Miller believed his one-alpha-per-pack mantra.

Cam looked around wildly for a way out, then suddenly a second huge man—he had to be another bodyguard—came barreling around the corner. He threw Miller up against the wall; a mirror shattered behind his back, and Cam forced aside the nasty thought that maybe Miller would get cut today after all.

The man must have heard the shots, Cam reasoned. He watched Miller hold his own with the much-larger bodyguard, blocking his punches, kneeing him hard in the groin.

And then Cam spotted the third bodyguard coming around the corner, his own AK-47 held confidently aloft.

Cam didn't have time to think; he threw his empty gun at the bodyguard, then tic-tacked off the wall as the bullets started flying toward where he'd been standing just seconds before.

The third bodyguard was a lot smaller than the guy who was still on Miller. An image of Nikki's face flashed into Cam's mind, and he put all his anger and resolution into his right hook. The guy crumpled.

He turned to see that the other bodyguard had Miller pinned to the ground. The small velvet bag went flying; one of them kicked it farther across the floor. Cam reached for the bag, and, for the first time in his messenger (or criminal) career, he looked inside.

It was filled with diamonds.

Cam had never been a lucky guy, but he knew how to take a break when he found one. *This* was Cam's exit plan. He gripped the bag tightly in his hand, closing his eyes for a moment, again thinking of Nikki.

Moving quickly, he made his way back up to the skylight. The glass had been supported by two steel beams; he used an end table to gain some extra height, leapt, and caught one of the beams, pulling himself up as if the beams were parallel bars.

He emerged just a few feet from Dylan, and couldn't help but notice the surprise on his face when he saw Cam standing there, still breathing.

Dylan drew his gun. "Don't . . . don't move," he stammered.

"Shoot him!" Miller called up to Dylan. "He's got the package." Cam looked down and saw that the bodyguard had Miller in a choke hold on the floor.

Dylan's hand shook as he aimed his gun. Cam could see the sweat on his forehead.

"Shoot him!" Miller yelled again.

Dylan and Cam exchanged a look. Decision time for Dylan. "Dylan, put the gun down," Cam said, reaching a hand toward him, trying to reason with him—this guy he'd thought of as a friend.

Dylan kept staring at him, clearly conflicted. Slowly, Dylan lowered his weapon.

They heard shots. Miller was back on his feet. The guy he'd been fighting wasn't moving. Miller had crossed the room and was standing below the skylight now, ready to fire on both of them.

Just then, the apartment door burst open with a loud crack. Miller turned to fire, quickly dropping at least three of his new attackers. Cam motioned to Dylan, and they both backed away from the skylight. Cam searched for the best way out. After a few seconds, he decided to leap across to the next building's roof. The sounds of gunfire were audible but fading as he landed.

He heard a thud behind him and glanced back to make sure it was Dylan who'd followed him.

But it was Miller.

The guy had been right about one thing: today would be a new plateau for Cam's tracing. He raced across the roof, covering it in seconds. The next roof was a bit lower; Cam jumped and rolled smoothly, rising up to keep running. He didn't spare another glance behind him, though he still heard footsteps.

Remembering his first job with the "family"—his initiation—Cam knew how hard Miller would be to shake. But he didn't have a choice. This wasn't a test or a game.

The next building had a narrow ledge he'd have to aim for, but Cam didn't waver or look down—just kept running. He caught a glimpse of Miller's dark blue coveralls as the older man made an impressive leap down, closing the distance between them.

Cam barely slowed as he spotted an open window on the side of the next building, just vaulted in and kept running—right through someone's apartment, up and over the couch, and out their front door. He found himself in the building's stairwell; he took the stairs five, six at a time, using the metal railings to stay on his feet.

Finally, Cam burst out through the service entrance and hit the street at a run. Even though he was sprinting full out, a plan was starting to form in his head.

He had only one chance.

He knew the city pretty well after being a bike messenger

for so long. He would head south—and hope that Miller wouldn't see it coming.

As he rounded the corner, he spotted a parked police cruiser. The cop had been getting back in the car, but he paused when he saw Cam race past.

Cam didn't stop. He heard Miller come up behind the cop and say, "DEA, I'm taking your car," like he was really proud of himself. Yeah, the guy was a pillar of the freaking community.

"No!" the cop yelled.

From the sound of squealing tires behind him, Cam guessed that Miller had taken the car in spite of the cop's protests. He ducked in closer to the buildings, trying not to let his former boss (attempted murder was definitely grounds for quitting) run him over.

He might not be able to commandeer a police car, but Cam made use of every other vehicle in his path, leaping from roof to roof, kong-vaulting faster than he ever had before. His lungs were on fire, the cut on his arm burned, but he tuned out everything except the idea of escape.

Abruptly, he ran out of vehicles to leap over, and he found himself back on the ground He looked up and saw Miller driving straight for him, determined to run him over.

But the car couldn't run up a wall. And Cam *could.* He tic-tacked up the wall of the closest building just as the car approached. Miller almost wiped out, squealing to a stop at the last second.

At that moment, a van T-boned the police car; both vehicles spun out.

It took Cam a few seconds to realize that it was the van he'd been riding in just an hour before.

Nikki.

He raced over and wrenched open the nearly fused door. "Are you okay?" he asked.

She nodded, clearly dazed. "Yeah."

"You have to get out of here," Cam said, breathing hard, putting a hand on her arm, almost not believing that she was real. He'd been silently calling to her across the city. But now that she was sitting there in front of him, all he wanted was for her to be out of there, to be safe. He helped her out of the van and they started to run.

"Stop!"

Cam turned at the sound of Miller's voice. The Energizer Bunny of evil had survived the crash and was back on his feet—bleeding and dazed, but still coming. Still holding a gun.

Cam moved to stand in front of Nikki.

"Give me the diamonds, Cam," Miller called.

They heard sirens in the distance.

"Stop it, James," Nikki yelled. "It's over."

He actually looked hurt by her words. "Okay, then. If that's how you want it." He raised his gun, aimed . . .

A motorcycle skidded to a stop not ten feet away from Miller. Cam took advantage of the brief distraction and grabbed Nikki's hand, leading her behind a row of parked cars.

"Stay with me," Cam told her. "Follow my lead."

They kept running, with Cam leading the way. His only hope, really, was that he'd led Miller on enough of a chase to prevent him from realizing where they were heading.

He spared one glance back. Miller was still right on their heels. Cam said a silent prayer as they reached their destination. He ran up to the building and pulled open the door. He exhaled in relief as the door opened. He gave Nikki a little push to send her inside, then backed in himself, with his hands up.

Miller burst in just after them, his gun raised.

"Dead end," he said, sounding pleased with himself. "Come on, Nikki. Move away. I don't want to hurt you."

Cam didn't normally find the sound of guns being

cocked to be a happy one, but at that moment it was like the sound of angels singing.

Out of the darkness, all around them, stepped the Tong. His old friends Jerry and Hu among them.

The huge open space had once been some kind of theater. There were still huge banners—red silk decorated with gold Chinese characters—hanging haphazardly from the ceiling and walls. Behind them, Cam knew, was an empty stage. He knew this place from one memorable day, and from a thousand nightmares that came after.

A voice came out of the darkness, speaking Mandarin. Cam caught the name *Hatcher*.

It was a woman's voice. Cam turned and was shocked to see the old woman from the fish store. Miller was staring at her in horror.

This, clearly, was Chen. The boss. Like an idiot, Cam had always assumed that Chen was some big, burly guy.

"Chen?" Miller's voice sounded completely different. He wasn't the alpha dog here.

No, Miller was the about-to-wet-himself runt of the litter here.

Chen kept speaking, still in Mandarin. It was obvious that Miller understood her; he answered her in the same language.

They switched to English. "There's been a mistake," Miller said.

"There *has* been a mistake," Chen agreed. "You have made it."

Miller was glaring at Cam. He couldn't help but smile back.

Chen was still speaking to Miller. "I told you a long time ago to stay out of my neighborhood."

Miller's voice came out breathless and panicked; all his bravado was gone. "I've honored your request, Chen. I kept my business away from yours. But this one's personal. Give me these two and you'll never see me again."

Chen was smiling. "Your business here is closed. You've been making too much trouble for too many of my friends. It's time for you to go away for a while."

"But, Chen . . ."

"You belong to me now, Agent Hatcher."

Cam's old friend Hu walked up to Miller, smiling as he took his gun and ripped the badge from around his neck.

Chen continued to regard Miller with a steady, unblinking gaze. "There's a boat leaving for Macau in two hours," she told him. "Mr. Hu will make sure you're on it. Some friends of mine want to talk to you. Say good-bye now, James."

Hu started to lead his captive back toward the exit, but

Miller lunged toward Nikki, his face a mask of anger. Hu held him back, but he couldn't stop him from yelling.

"After everything I did for you? How long are you gonna last without me, Nikki? How long?"

Nikki blinked away tears, but didn't look away from Miller. She didn't give him an answer either.

Miller had expected an answer, Cam saw. He watched as the remaining fight went out of the man; he seemed to shrink several inches before their eyes.

Hu smiled as he slid a black bag over Miller's head. Another gangster grabbed Miller's other arm and they led him out.

Cam watched them take Miller away. Some part of him couldn't quite believe that his crazy plan had actually worked. He couldn't believe how much had changed since that morning, when Miller had been confidently planning to kill him and leave town with Nikki and the others.

Pulling Cam out of his reverie, Chen turned to him and asked, "You have something for me?"

Cam nodded and handed her the pouch of diamonds. She looked inside, carefully taking inventory and smiling.

And then something unbelievable happened. She took out one diamond and flicked it back to Cam.

"Your debt is clear. Don't ever come back to Chinatown."

First Miller was gone. Then, moments later, his debt was gone too. Cam suddenly felt light enough to fly—the heavy weight that had been pressing on him for months had lifted. He turned to Nikki and saw that her radiant smile mirrored his own.

She took a step closer and threaded her fingers through his. Cam looked down at their intertwined hands and squeezed. For the first time in years, maybe in his life, he was filled with something he thought was probably hope.

Cam looked up to see Chen walk out of the theater, with the others falling in line behind her.

Jerry hung back. Cam walked up and found him smiling too. "You're one lucky bastard, Cam. That's the best deal I ever seen anybody cut with Chen."

"What about *our* deal?" he asked. Extreme good fortune had made Cam bold.

Jerry stared at him for a few seconds, then his face broke out into a wider grin. "All right. Your debt *is* clear. What the hell? I could use the karma points." He tossed Cam the keys. Not a bad guy, in spite of all the death threats.

Together, he and Nikki walked back out into the sunlight, their hands still clasped tight. The whole world looked different in that moment: the colors were brighter. He could hear birds singing, a sound he hadn't noticed in what seemed like years. The GTO was parked across the street from the warehouse. Cam felt the weight of the keys in his hand. He caught Nikki's eye. She was grinning back at him.

He had done it. He'd found their exit strategy.

Cam opened the passenger door for Nikki, let go of her hand, then vaulted over the hood and slid into the driver's seat. He turned the key and sighed with pleasure to hear it start up purring. His car was running perfectly.

He looked over at Nikki. "Where to?"

She leaned her head back against the seat and smiled back at him. "Let's just drive."

NINETEEN

CAM GOT in the lane for the Holland Tunnel—heading out of the city. He looked over at Nikki as she sat back in her seat, a peaceful smile on her face.

"I have one more debt to settle," he told her. She frowned a little, but nodded. Cam pulled out his phone and dialed the number he'd saved yesterday. Angie picked up after just two rings.

"Cam? Please tell me you're calling with good news."

He smiled so widely he thought maybe Angie could see it across the phone connection. "It's good news. All clear. You can go home."

"Oh, Cam—how? Wait, never mind. I don't want to know. But . . . you're sure? Completely positive?"

"One hundred percent. And, Angie? I'm really sorry. Again. For everything."

"I'm just glad it's over and you're safe. And *we're* safe! Mostly that last part," she added, laughing.

He laughed too. "Just stay at your old address long enough for me to send you a package, yeah?"

"Cam, you don't owe . . ."

"I know what I owe, Ang," he said, cutting her off. "And I always pay my debts."

It was really nice to be able to say those words.

"Who was that?" Nikki asked, after Cam hung up.

As he pulled up to a red light, he looked over at her, still grinning. "What, are you jealous?"

She crossed her arms. "No."

"Well, good. Because that was my landlady. She was a friend of my mom's. I kind of jammed her up in my trouble with the Tong. I had to let her know I was in the clear."

"Oh. Well, that's good."

"So there's nothing else to delay our getting the hell out of here," Cam said, looking over at her once again. "You do still want that?" He felt the air catch in his lungs; he was holding his breath waiting for her answer.

Her eyes met his for a second. "I do," she said. "But . . ."

Cam exhaled. "But . . ."

"I texted Dylan. I need to see him."

They were still at the red light, and Cam turned fully to face her. "This *actual* morning, your brother came this close to shooting me. You do realize that?" He demonstrated the narrow margin of Dylan's decision by holding his thumb and index finger so close together they were almost touching.

Nikki held his stare, looking determined. "But he *didn't* shoot you."

Cam frowned back at her. "True."

"He's my brother, Cam."

Cam groaned. "Are you trying to tell me he's coming with us?"

"No." Her voice sounded sad, but resigned. "He's going home."

"Home? What about his 'trouble'?"

"The kid's big-shot actor dad OD'd. It was on the news just the other day. And, last I heard, a scholarship got the kid himself out of Florida—I don't think Dylan will have to worry about running into him there. Now he can go back. It's all he ever really wanted."

"Do I need to turn around?"

"Yes. He's meeting us in the cell-phone lot at JFK."

Cam turned around and headed for the Verrazano Bridge. They rode the rest of the way to the airport in silence. Nikki spotted her brother waiting at the edge of the lot and pointed. Cam pulled the GTO up beside him.

Dylan was standing with the hood of his black sweatshirt pulled over his head, even though it was warm and sunny out. Nikki leapt out of the car as soon as Cam came to a stop. Dylan picked her up and held her in midair for a few seconds before letting go.

Cam got out of the car, putting his hands in his pockets. He felt like an intruder in this moment between them.

"You're sure Miller's gone?" Dylan asked Nikki as they broke apart.

She nodded. "Yes. It's all over. He's definitely gone."

"But what do you mean *gone*?" Dylan asked sharply. "Define *gone.*"

Cam noticed then that Dylan's eyes were red rimmed, and he needed a shave. Maybe he'd been more upset about executing Miller's plan than Cam had thought.

"How about Macau?" Nikki replied. "That gone enough for you?"

Her brother shook his head. "I have no idea where that is."

"Neither do I. But I know it's on the other side of the world."

Dylan stepped away from Nikki and looked over at Cam. He opened his mouth, swallowed hard, then took another deep breath before speaking. "Look, Cam, I know . . . I owe you an apology, man."

"For leading me toward certain death?" Cam shrugged. "Bygones."

Dylan shifted his weight uncomfortably. "I didn't know what to do . . ." He seemed to be fumbling for the right words. "Miller told me what would happen to Niks if I didn't . . ."

"I get it," Cam said, cutting him off. "I know what you were up against, man. I really do. And when it came to decision time, you didn't shoot me. Even though it might have meant something bad happening to you or Nikki. So I mean it: bygones. Seriously. We're good." Cam extended his hand, and Dylan took it, smiling gratefully.

Nikki was smiling too, as she looked from Cam to her brother. Her face changed a few seconds later, when the sound of a low-flying plane filled the air. "You're really leaving?" she asked Dylan.

"Are *you*?" Dylan shot back, giving Cam a significant look.

Nikki didn't hesitate: "Yes."

"I'm going home, Niks," Dylan confirmed. "I can finally go home. I've already talked to Mom, and to Allison."

"Allison's still single?" Nikki asked, grinning. "Did she wait all this time for you?"

Dylan's face changed. He looked younger suddenly—and very happy. "I can't believe it either. I'll give Mom your love?"

There was a momentary hesitation, but Nikki nodded again. "Yeah."

The two siblings hugged again, Dylan wiping quickly at his eyes. Nikki wasn't bothering to hide her tears. "Take care of yourself—and Mom. Like you always took care of me, okay?"

Dylan broke away from Nikki first, giving Cam another handshake and asking him to look out for his sister.

"Is Tate okay?" Cam asked.

Dylan nodded. "Yeah. He's staying here. This is home for him. He's gonna lay low until things quiet down."

"Hey, what about Jax's dogs? We can't just leave them . . ."

Dylan held up a hand. "Chill, Cam. Tate's keeping them."

"He didn't really seem like a dog person."

"Nah, it's cool, guy's all talk. Besides, I think they remind him of Jax, you know?"

Cam nodded. "Makes sense."

Nikki gave her brother one more quick hug, then broke away from him and climbed back into the car. Dylan offered a wave and started walking toward the terminal.

"Stay outta trouble!" Nikki called to him.

Dylan waved once more, then turned around and kept walking.

Cam sat behind the wheel, steering the car back into the traffic heading out of the city.

"So where to?" he asked, more to distract Nikki than anything else.

She wiped at her eyes with the sleeve of her T-shirt. "We're going home too."

Cam gave her a surprised smile. "I know you don't mean back to New York . . ."

Nikki shook her head.

"And you just cried all over your brother, who's headed back to *your* hometown . . ."

"No, that's not where I meant either. Come on, Cam. You'll figure it out . . ."

"I give up."

"We're heading to this little town in SoCal. It's called Lone Pine. You know . . . where your mom is from."

"You remembered?"

"I did more than that." She pulled out her phone and started tapping. "At the next red light, you have to see this."

A minute or so later, Cam hit the brakes and took Nikki's phone.

The screen showed the Chamber of Commerce website for Lone Pine. Cam smiled at her. She'd obviously done some research of her own.

He looked down to see a picture of a perfect blue sky dotted with bright white clouds. Jagged white rocks jutted up from the ground. And perched in midair hung a man wearing a black T-shirt and baggy cargoes.

There it was, right there on the Lone Pine website: parkour.

"It's our destiny!" she told him.

Cam handed the phone back. "When did you find this?"

She smiled back at him. "The day after you told me about where your mom grew up."

"Destiny," he repeated. "I like the sound of that."

"Me too."

ACKNOWLEDGMENTS

SO MANY THANKS go out to my phenomenal agent, Suzie Townsend, and to the whole gang at New Leaf, with a special shout-out to the awesome Danielle Barthel. Thank you guys so much for reading, believing, and for all the invaluable notes.

Thank you to my amazing editor, Shauna Rossano, who is always supportive and cheerful (even when we have to do math!), and to Jen Besser and the whole Putnam team.

Thank you to Marty Bowen and everyone at Temple Hill. Special thanks go out to Pete Harris for bringing me on board with such a great project—and for loving the action scenes!

Thank you to my school family for supporting me as I continue on this writing journey, and to my students, who keep me entertained, inspired, and humble.

Finally, thank you to my chicas, for all the love, support, and appetizers.